DULCE TRUTHS

The Dulce Files, Book Two

GREG STRANDBERG

Big Sky Words Press, Missoula

Big Sky Words

First paperback printing, 2018

Printed in the United States of America

ISBN: 9781726660624

CONTENTS

PRELUDE – THE ENTRANCE

The Jicarilla Indian Reservation near Dulce, New Mexico
August 9, 1947

Noro continues up the trail, finally coming to its rocky top. He stands there on the ridge, surveying the vast Archuleta Mesa. It's a rocky landscape, with scrub bushes here and there, sometimes a patch of juniper trees, but mostly jagged rocks the color of burnt orange. It was the land Noro had called home for all his 62 years. He was a Jicarilla Apache Indian, with hair still long and still quite black. It blew in the wind, though the yellow bandana tied around his forehead kept the hair out of his eyes. He'd surveyed his homeland many times, but for the others with him it was new ground. Noro stood waiting for those others to come up behind him. Colonel Harry Anderholt was first.

"There it is," Noro says, putting his arm up to point out the area.

"Where?" Anderholt says.

"There…by those large boulders…you can't see it from here, but once you get there you'll be able to walk behind them."

"And that's where the entrance is?"

Noro nods but continues to look out at the rocks in the distance. "The bones mark it, bones that've been sitting there for 60 years…ever since we came to this land." He looks back to Anderholt. "We Jicarilla know enough to stay away from that place, you should too."

Anderholt puts his arm up. "Lead on."

Noro was expecting such a response, and simply turns back around and starts down the trail. His mind starts down the trail of memories.

The Jicarilla Apache called Dulce home, had for nearly a hundred years. The tribe spoke the Southern Athabaskan language, though the name 'Jicarilla' was actually Mexican Spanish, meaning "little basket." Hundreds of years ago they'd been located in the Sangre de Cristo Mountains, in what would eventually become the state of Colorado. Beginning around the year 1525, however, they began to branch out into the Great Plains. For about 175 years they lived the life of plains Indians, riding their horses and hunting the buffalo, until the eastern tribes were pushed ever westward by the whites and their expansions inland. The Jicarilla were pushed south into the less-hospitable lands surrounding the Archuleta Mesa, an area that'd eventually become part of New Mexico. Years of smallpox and tuberculosis followed and the tribe was decimated. Then in 1887 they were given their reservation and 20 years after that they were allowed to expand into the lush San Juan Basin. Finally, things began to look up for the tribe. It didn't last long.

By 1920 most of the tribal members were suffering from either malnutrition or tuberculosis. It was widely believed that the tribe would go extinct. To make matters worse, the reliable pastime of sheepherding fell on hard times. Many tribal members gave up on the land and moved to town. The closest was Dulce, which at that point had but a few hundred people. The Gomez family had started the place as a ranching stronghold in 1877, naming it "Agua Dulce", Spanish for "sweet water." A natural spring ran through the area, giving the people and the animals a reliable source of drinking water in the parched land. Then WWII came, taking a few of the Indians and town folk as recruits. For the most part the war had little impact on that corner of the country, though the area *was* eyed for its resource potential. That's how things got started – with lumber.

The Jicarilla had been looking for some lumber to help them build their homes, for while the government might have allowed for a reservation back in the 1880s, it sure didn't allow for much funding to help get it up and running. So the Indians relied on themselves, and the land around them, just as they had for centuries. That's how a small group of them chanced upon the cave. Their bones were still there.

The Jicarilla had told the government, but the government hadn't cared. *Something mysterious killing Indians? Why, that'll just make our job easier!* Noro imagines that was the response in whatever department in Washington was in charge back then. No, the government hadn't been interested then, but they were sure interested now. All the flying craft that'd been seen in the area lately had a lot to do with that. Just the month before, Noro knew, one of those craft had crashed 300 miles to the south of them, in a sleepy little town called Roswell. Noro wasn't sure what had happened with that crash exactly, but ever since then there'd been more and more government and military types poking around the reservation near Dulce.

One of those military types was Colonel Anderholt.

The colonel was in his early-30s. He had short brown hair without a hint of grey in it and a firm face that looked chiseled, as did his body. He'd been in the Army ever since FDR had started the home study Army extension courses back in 1935. That'd allowed him a leg-up on joining the reserves before his 18th birthday, which didn't come until the following year. After that it'd been the standard rigors until mobilization for WWII had started. Due to Anderholt's high aptitude test scores, he was chosen for the Office of Strategic Services, or OSS, even before it officially started in 1942. That'd limited his combat roles in Europe while increasing his intelligence gathering work. When the OSS was rolled into the CIA after the war, Anderholt was one of the first to start at the new agency. He also took on the rank of Master Sergeant in the Air Force, a sly bit of bureaucratic rigmarole that gave him even more power and influence. From there it was work with Majestic 12 – or MJ12 as it was called – and that's the reason he'd been sent to the Four Corners region, specifically New Mexico.

The general saw things much differently, and as they walked down that rocky trail he could picture what the area would become, and how.

Just a couple weeks before, after all, the government had crafted a faux story about a lumber company building a logging road through Dulce to get at the pine, fir, and spruce trees of the nearby San Juan National Forest. The trucks that went in and out were all labeled with "Smith Corp." on the side, a 'company' based out of Paragosa Springs, Colorado. No lumber was ever hauled on the road, however, though sometimes late at night people would report seeing the trucks loaded down with big equipment destined for some area close by. Now Dulce Base had a path to it, though eventually that logging road would be destroyed. It was all part of the vast plan that MJ12 had put into place, and Anderholt had been chosen to see it through.

How long the 'base' was there before the government got ready to refit it into a high-tech military installation was anyone's guess, the colonel figured. Some say it'd been there for thousands of years, an entrance to the vast underground world where secret alien races lived, and had been living for eons. One story had the secret society known as the Illuminati entering into a pact with these alien nations beginning in 1933, and soon the government officials the society handled were trading humans and animals for high-tech know-how.

Power would be needed to run those high-tech gadgets, Anderholt knew. To supply it, much of what the nearby Navajo Dam produced would be diverted to Dulce. In case the need for backup power arose, the El Vado Dam would be selected as a standby, and as a second location for an entrance to Dulce. Most of this work would conducted by the Rand Corporation, with help from Bechtel.

Much of Dulce and its tunnel system, and the bases around the world just like it, would be constructed with "the Subterrene," a nuclear-powered tunnel machine that burrows through the deep, underground rock by heating whatever stone it encounters into molten rock. This rock then cools as the machine passes and the tunnels it creates have a smooth, glazed lining.

Where would all that extra rock go that the Subterrene pushes forth before it? Why, into the lakes around the El Vado Dam! Heron Lake…El Vado Lake…Stone Lake…Horse Lake…Stinking Lake…all would be created under the guise of grants for the Indians. While the area Indians would get *some* work blasting and hauling rock to make the lakes and dams and reservoirs, in reality they'd just be pawns. The lakes would be underwater launch sites for aliens, and disposal areas for the tons of molten rock that the underground tunnel excavations created.

Thirty minutes after starting down from the ridge, Noro reaches the boulders that he'd pointed out. As usual, Anderholt is right behind him, the other dozen or so men bringing up the rear. Each has a machine gun shouldered. Noro knows the guns won't be enough. *Tanks wouldn't be*, he thinks.

"Well, what are you waiting for?" Anderholt asks.

"I'll go no further," Noro says, "no Jicarilla Indian will."

"*You'll go no…*" Anderholt starts before trailing-off. He then crosses his arms over his chest and gives Noro an angry stare. "I'm *paying* you to go further, all the way in fact!"

Noro shakes his head. "No amount of money'll be enough."

"Money won't, eh?" Anderholt says as he uncrosses his arms and lowers one down to his side, never taking his eyes from Noro's. His fingers wrap around the handle of the Walther P38 he'd taken from a dead Nazi in a Berlin bunker years before. He slowly draws it from its holster then brings the weapon up and levels it at Noro, who's standing just six feet away. "Then maybe this will," he finishes.

Noro straightens, firming-up his stance while keeping his eyes locked on Anderholt's. The men are of equal height, though vastly different experiences. Anderholt is a man of war, having fought in one and now overseeing the start of what'd likely be countless others. Noro, on the other hand, is a man of peace and the earth. He seeks way to resolve conflicts while Anderholt blindly charges forth, eager to create them. *And am I ready to die for those beliefs?* Noro thinks to himself as Anderholt continues to point that gun at him. The answer comes quickly: *Yes.*

Noro was about to voice that thought – in a vehement, "No!" that he expected would earn him the bullet that'd earn him his death, but instead a force seems to take him over and the words are unable to come out. He wants to speak out, but can't. What he *can* do, and what his body seems to want to do against his own will, is turn around and continue on the last short bit to the entrance of the cave.

Lead him, a voice comes to Noro, a voice not his own. He narrows his eyes and glances from Anderholt to the other soldiers gathered about. None looked to have said a thing.

Noro looks back at Anderholt, his resolve to say, "No!" all the stronger. He manages to take a step forth to say the word, and although his mouth quivers with the effort of getting it out, nothing comes out.

Lead him…or die, the voice in Noro's head comes again, and this time it's accompanied by worst headache the Indian's ever experienced. So strong is it that he sways on his feet, and nearly falls to his knees. He would have, he realizes a moment later when he's able to open his eyes, had Anderholt not rushed forth to latch onto his arm.

"You alright?" the colonel says, a concerned look on his face. Noro can barely focus on that face, however, so searing is the memory of the pain in his mind. It lasted for only a second or two, but seemed a lifetime.

Lead him…the voice comes again, and this time Noro does focus on Anderholt's face. He knows he's the 'him' that *they're* referring to.

"Noro?" Anderholt says, his eyes narrowed, though Noro now thinks the concern in them is more for the mission, not for his condition.

"I'll take you to the entrance, no further," Noro says in a shaky voice as he begins to push himself up. Anderholt takes one arm to help him.

"That's all I ever asked," the colonel says.

Noro nods to that and the small group starts down the trail once again. It takes them another few minutes to reach the boulders that Noro had pointed out from the ridge but then they're there, and Noro is looking none too happy about it.

"All the way," Anderholt says as the Indian stalls a bit, looking around instead of going behind the final boulder.

Lead him, the voice comes to Noro once again, and with it the slightest of sharp pains behind his temples. With a frown at Anderholt, Noro turns and heads to that final boulder.

It's large but behind it is a slight crack, a sort of opening that perhaps two people can slip through at a time. Noro stalls again, but some loose rocks skittering behind him tells him that Anderholt is right there, likely with that gun of his still out and ready to use. Noro moves on, despite his better judgment, and passes behind the boulder.

Then he's in, right at the opening to a *very* large cave. Its ceiling is high and the walls are spaced more than twenty feet apart. That's not what Noro notices most, however. No, what really catches his eye are the bones on the floor, a large pile of them, perhaps a dozen or so men. Noro knows they're Indian bones, those of his ancestors. Bits of decaying feather headdresses and the occasional arrowhead stick out here and there. Skulls stare out with empty eye sockets and wide, often toothless mouths. They look to be screaming, every single one of them that Noro can see.

The Jicarilla still speak of the legends when they occasionally gather around the fires on spring and summer nights. They speak of the daring braves that went forth long ago to look in the cave of evil, the cave of nightmares, the cave of…*them.* Noro knows he's looking at those braves from long ago, and then a slight movement catches his eye from further down the cave. At that point he knows he's looking at what killed those braves, he's looking at *them.*

"My God!" Anderholt says behind him, though Noro doesn't turn around. His eyes are locked on the same thing that Anderholt's are – a large, spindly-armed creature walking toward them, large black eyes staring out from the head on its narrow neck. It has no clothes, nor any kind of sexual features. It barely has a mouth! What it does have, however, is a *presence* about it, a command authority that seems to take hold of Noro and Anderholt both, bowing them to its will. And then it speaks, though not with that tiny mouth, but with its mind.

Your kind is not to come here, you know this.

The thought is directed to Noro, but Anderholt can hear it as well and Noro knows it.

"I…I…" Noro manages to stutter, but that's all. Without raising a finger or even moving at all, for all Anderholt can see, the Gray lashes out somehow at Noro. Perhaps it's with its mind, or some other power. Either way, Noro begins to lift off the ground a foot or two, his feet kicking all the while as some unseen force latches onto his throat. It has to be there, Anderholt thinks, for the poor bastard is lashing and clawing there, as if some fist has hold of him. It does no good, other than to scratch away at the skin, which even causes some bleeding. Anderholt can only watch with wide eyes as it happens, as Noro is choked to death.

Then it's done, and the unseen force holding Noro up lets him go. The Indian slams down to the floor near the pile of bones, his eyes wide and his mouth open in what looks like a silent scream.

Anderholt's eyes go back to the alien in front of him, a Gray, he knows. It's not just one though, he sees now, as another is visible, and another over by the side. He thinks there's probably a lot more hidden away in the darkness further down that tunnel. The general stands stock still, his eyes wide and his hands out to his sides in a sort of stabilizing, defensive gesture. It was a stance that said, 'whoa…what just happened here, and how can we make sure it doesn't happen again?'

Perhaps the Grays read into that stance, or perhaps they just read Anderholt's mind. Either way, come the next moment the Grays seemed to relax, and all at once. The men watched as the aliens' posture became less erect and their eyes became a bit smaller. It seemed that way, at least, and Anderholt figured that now was the time. He began to lower his arms, and made ready to step forward.

Stay, a voice comes to him, one that isn't audible but which he can hear in his head. Anderholt tenses up, and doesn't take that step. Instead he decides to just start talking.

Quiet, the voice comes again, and this time Anderholt turns and looks over his shoulder at the men behind him. Their eyes narrow at him, as if wondering what he's doing, but not a one says a word. Anderholt wonders if any heard what he'd just heard.

They did not, the voice answered, *nor will they. You're in command here. We'll talk to you…for now.*

That startled the colonel and put him off-guard. He looks back at the aliens, their faces expressionless, those large eyes showing a deep blackness and hinting at nothing else.

I'm – the colonel started to think, but his thoughts were interrupted.

General Anderholt, the voice in his head answers for him, *born 1918, joined the military in 1936,, served in World War II from 1938 to 1945, and for the past two years in charge of the secret alien collection unit of the CIA.*

Anderholt cocks his head to one side in a kind of shrug that says, 'not bad.'

What do you want? the voice comes again. *You shouldn't be here.*

Why not? Anderholt thinks.

Because it'll be the death of you, Harry.

Anderholt frowns to that. *The American government is strong, our military–*

We're not talking about your government or your military…we're talking about you, Harry.

That frazzles Anderholt. *You know how I'm gonna die?*

Of course. But colonel…would you *like to know?*

Anderholt immediately thinks 'no,' but at the same time another part of him thought 'yes.' It must have been that part that the aliens latched-onto, or else they were going to tell him regardless.

It'll be 32 years from now, Harry, deep down in the depths of the base you'll see built here, the voice says. *We're not worried about telling you this, either, for there's nothing you can do to change it.*

So the future's already set in stone then, is it? Anderholt thinks to himself, and before he could think not to.

The colonel thinks he detects a trace of humor in the voice's next response. *For you, colonel, yes.*

Anderholt stares back at the few Grays standing there, looking deeply into those large, black eyes. Behind him the men begin to grow antsy, and Anderholt can hear them beginning to shuffle about. He puts up his hand to signal that everything is alright, though privately he thinks, *is it?*

Whether the Grays read that thought or not, Anderholt doesn't know. Perhaps they chose to ignore it. Anderholt has no way of knowing either way, but one thing he does know – he won't be dying here, at least not today. That thought fills him with a sense of confidence, boosting his courage, and making him realize that there was nothing to worry about. *He* was in charge, and he'd act like it.

'The base I'll see built here' you said, Anderholt thinks, trying his best to direct it toward the Grays. *If that's the case, then get out of my way and let me build it.*

Anderholt keeps his gaze locked on the Gray closest to him, wondering if a thing with no eyelids could be stared down. He receives his answer a moment later when, without a word – or thought in this case – the Grays simply turn and begin to walk away down the long tunnel. After 40 yards or so wall lights end and the blackness swallows them up.

"Sir..." one of the men behind him says, "…what just happened?"

Anderholt turns around to look at the man, and the dozen or so others with him. "We've made contact, gentlemen…did you hear them talking to me with their thoughts?" No one speaks, but nearly everyone shakes their head 'no.' The colonel nods. "Didn't think so."

"Now what, sir?"

Anderholt turns and looks back down that long, dark tunnel. *What is down there,* he thinks, *and how will it kill me?* The Grays had said 32 years from now. That'd be 1979. Anderholt is 30 now. *I've got time*, he thinks, and then turns back to look at the men, and also to move toward them. They straighten up as he does so.

"Men, let's file out."

"Sir?" one of them says, alarmed. After all, they'd just spent so much time getting into the place, *and* had lost their guide.

Anderholt stops and looks at the soldier, then the others. "We've got a lot of equipment to bring in here if we mean to get this base started. Let's get a move-on."

He begins walking again, to the soldiers and then past them. He doesn't look back as he starts back to the cave's entrance…he knows he doesn't need to. Nothing is going to harm Colonel Anderholt for some time. There was nothing to be afraid of…yet.

PART I
1 – THE BACK DOOR

Dulce Tunnels (Level 5)
Friday, May 25, 1979
12:15 AM

Turn continues to stare at the two in front of him, especially this new man named Bennewitz. The three of them are running for all they're worth – well, not Turn, as his cybernetic legs would've taken him right past the other two without a sweat – for they know that up five levels at the base's entrance, Stu is there with his CED device. Any minute now and the whole place will be demolished, those upper levels and even those way down here, where the tube trains run and where they'd find a path to another base.

Turn still couldn't believe what he'd just seen minutes before – Aaron pulling his knife from Johnny's chest. Why Aaron would kill a fellow teammate, Turn didn't know, but he knew he had to find out. If he didn't, more of his teammates would die. *But how many are just like Aaron*, he thinks*, traitors in our midst, just waiting to stick the knife in?*

"Guys, I've gotta tell you something…" Turn starts to say, the three of them still running.

"It isn't about that traitor Aaron Haney, is it?" Paul says over his shoulder.

"How…how'd you know?" Turn asks.

Paul looked back over his shoulder at Turn, a sly smile on his face. He was a wild-eyed man with red, curly hair and shining white teeth.

Turn didn't know if he could trust him…didn't know if he could trust *anyone* anymore.

"There's a lot of things Paul here knows," Walter says, not looking back, "and the big reason for that is how much time travelling he's done."

"*Whoa!*" Turn says, slowing and then stopping completely. The other two had no choice but to stop as well, to turn and look back at Turn. "This is gettin' a little *too* damn weird." He shakes his head and crosses his arms. "I need some answers."

"Turn, this base is gonna blow in…" Walter looks over at Paul, who in turn looks down at his watch.

"Seven minutes," Paul says, glancing back up at Turn.

"I need some answers," Turn says, his jaw firm and those arms of his still crossed defiantly across his chest.

"Bloody hell!" Walter says, turning away with a roll of his eyes, but Bennewitz only nods his head and steps forward.

"Like I said, the name's Paul Bennewitz," the man says, looking over his shoulder at Turn, "…that doesn't ring a bell?"

"Sure don't," Turn says as they continue to rush down the smoothed-out tunnels.

"When were you *born*?" Bennewitz says, giving another look over his shoulder. When Turn just screws up his face in confusion, however, he shakes his head and waves his hand. "Never mind. What I'm trying to say is–"

"What Paul here's trying to say," Walter cuts in from in front of them, still running but speaking in such a way that you'd never know it, "is that he feels he should be famous, well-known…a *household* name, if you will." Walter smirks and looks at Bennewitz. "Isn't that right, Paul?"

"It *is* right…just not in this here and now."

Turn's eyes narrow at that, and he's about to throw out another question – or twenty – but suddenly the tunnel turns and they're face to face with a group of Reptilians.

"Whoa!" Turn says, startled by the sight. The way the Reptilians jumped when they saw him, he thought they might be feeling the same way.

"Give it to 'em!" Walter shouts as he starts firing with his AR-15 Assault Rifle.

The tunnel is suddenly filled with the sound of bullets flying. Turn watches as one of the Reptilians is hit, then another as Walter strafes them. He gets his own gun up and takes one down himself. The Reptilians are going for their own guns, but being as surprised as they are, they just can't do it. Walter rips into them and Turn does too. Within seconds the half dozen Reptilians are down to just a couple. Then Turn see's Bennewitz's hand go up beside him, a flash gun in it.

ZAP!

Bennewitz fires and the second to last Reptilians is winked from existence, nothing more than a small pile of ash to show it ever walked the earth. Its final companion begins to hiss and shriek, but that lasts but a moment before a hail of bullets from Walter's gun takes it in the head.

Paul looks down at his watch again when the firing is done. "Six minutes," he says, "we gotta go."

"*Six…*" Turn starts to say, then slaps his hand down on his thigh in frustration. "Where the hell we supposed to go in six minutes?"

"Not *where*, but *when*," Bennewitz says to him, and then continues on past the pile of dead Reptilians.

Turn gives Walter a narrow-eyed, skeptical look, but the captain just shrugs.

"C'mon," he says, starting after Bennewitz, "we don't have much time."

With a roll of his eyes and a look over his shoulder – *and* the realization that he really can't do anything else – Turn follows.

2 – OFF THE GRID

They move the rest of the way down the tunnel they're in, then when a branch comes, Bennewitz ushers them to the left.

"Won't be much further," he shouts over his shoulder, looking down at his watch as he does so. The men keep up a steady jog, a pace that's conducive to talking. Turn still wants answers, so begins asking his questions again.

"You said time travel back there…right?"

"Thinkin' we can't be serious, right?" Walter says as the two run alongside one another. Bennewitz is just a few feet in front of them, but can hear their words as well. The tunnels are smooth and narrow, much like cave walls, and sound carries quite well.

"Well we *are* serious, no matter how much you think we might be joking," the wild-eyed man with red, curly hair says.

Turn rolls his eyes as he continues running. "Well, like you said back there…we got six minutes, so pray tell…what the hell's goin' on here, huh?"

Beside him Walter chuckles. "Better tell it to him from the top, Paul."

"Alrighty…here goes," Bennewitz says over his shoulder so Turn can hear. "I was 23-years-old when my interest in the UFO-phenomenon began. That's when I saw the report detailing the 500 UFOs that were spotted over the town of Dulce back in 1950. They were all in the sky at the same time, all making sharp, 90-degree turns at amazing angles." He pauses and shakes his head, looking down at the floor as he runs and perhaps back to those days more than twenty years ago. "I began to investigate, going to Dulce myself in the early-60s, eventually getting my pilot's license so I could see more. News spread of my…'research.' By the 70s I was getting photos from inside the base and just a few years ago I completed a full electronic surveillance of it. It was also around that time that I began investigating the cattle mutilations along with the Gomez ranching family. And of course I talked to the Jicarilla Apache to learn all they knew."

Up ahead another fork in the tunnel appears, and this time the men go right.

"Won't be much further," Walter says as they round the corner, but Turn hardly hears him. He's trying to process what Bennewitz has just said, and he's finding that he can't. *Time travel?* Ha – *that's children's story stuff there!* Still, Turn can't quite shake the feeling that what the man in front of him is saying is true. What he's seen over the past few hours in Dulce, after all, makes him realize that *anything* is possible.

"So you say 1950," Turn says as a lull comes in Bennewitz's telling, "but how long have the Grays been here, really?"

"The standard telling is that Dulce Base started up in '47," Bennewitz says.

"Which puts it eight years before Ike had his meeting with the Grays at Holloman," Walter says.

"But…I thought that was when we signed the treaty," Turn says. "Grays weren't supposed to have any bases before then, right…most of all not with the U.S. government."

Up ahead, Bennewitz shrugs. "Let's not forget that it was Truman that created Majestic 12, not Eisenhower. And let's also not forget that Ike met with three Pleiadians at California's Edwards Air Force Base in '54…a full year before the meeting at Holloman."

"But did he know about Dulce?" Turn asks

"I'm getting there," Bennewitz says over his shoulder, a little perturbed by the sound of it. "Now, a year after the first meeting with the Nordics, Ike has a *second* meeting with them. This time it's at Holloman Air Force Base in New Mexico. Air Force One lands, Ike tells the tower to turn off their radar, and then just like that, three UFOs appear. One lands, one hovers as a lookout, and one takes off from view. Ike gets off his plane and heads into the landed UFO, stays in there for a full 45 minutes." Bennewitz lets out a sigh then, something that's not so easy when running. "Let's just say that nothing went right. The Pleiadians – like most peaceful aliens in the universe – wanted us to stop our nuclear weapons tests. In exchange, they'd negotiate some sort of positive settlement to the Earth's problems."

"But it didn't happen that way," Walter says, and up ahead, Turn can see Bennewitz nodding.

"Nope, sure didn't," the wild-eyed man says. "Instead Ike signed a treaty with the Grays, mainly because he wanted their technology…something he figured the Ruskies didn't have. It's a shame, too, because the Pleiadians – sometimes called Nordics, mind you – wanted to help us *get rid of* the Grays." He laughs. "Boy, sure coulda used their help today, huh?"

"I guess what I'm wondering," Turn says, "is how'd it all go so wrong? How'd we go from peaceful relations to twenty years later shooting it out in these tunnels?"

"Treaty was broken by the Grays," Walter says beside him, "and in many ways. First, they were supposed to stay out of our affairs and we theirs. That's easy enough for us – we can't travel to *their* planet – but they've been embroiled in our politics for more than a decade now, ever since Kennedy was killed." He shrugs. "Their promise to give us some technology was kept, though I personally feel that they've held out on the good stuff."

"Ha, you've got that right!" Paul says from up ahead.

"As far as we know they haven't made a treaty with any other nations on Earth, which was part of the deal. The public hasn't been informed of them, which was another. The real clincher however, are the abductions. The original treaty that Eisenhower signed said that the Grays could abduct humans for various experiments, but that they'd also have to provide the names of every person they took. At first the Grays abided by this, telling MJ12 of all the humans they abducted and did God knows what on. But that all stopped in the early-60s, again, around the time Kennedy was killed."

"What was so special about that time?" Turn asks.

"It's when our government was stolen from us," Bennewitz says, "and a shadow government put in its place. No longer is the president in charge – those days are *long* behind us."

It was a lot to digest, all that Turn was hearing, and despite the numerous questions in his mind, he couldn't seem to put any into words. It was probably for the better – he wasn't sure he wanted to know it all, though he knew that wasn't true, either. Turn wanted to know it all, every last bit…and he had a feeling the two men he was with were just the people to tell him.

That telling would have to wait for another time, however. Another fork in the tunnel appears, they go left this time, and about a hundred yards down it they finally find something – a door.

"This is it," Bennewitz says as they reach it, "the time shed." He looks down at his watch as he says it. "Just in time, too – three minutes."

"Damn, I hope she's warmed up," Walter says as he goes to the door and makes to open it.

Bennewitz chuckles. "Oh, she's *always* warm."

Walter gets his hand on the metal doorknob, turns it, and pulls the door open. There before them is nothing more than a shimmering curtain of light, though that's not quite right either. If Turn had to describe it as anything he'd say it looked like one of those rain puddles you'd see at a gas station, an oil sheen floating at the top and giving the water a purplish, greenish sort of look.

"What…what…what the hell *is* that thing?"

"That, my friend," Walter says as he claps Turn on the shoulder, "is the time machine."

"And it's time we get in 'er," Bennewitz says, then glances to Walter. "I'll see you on the other side."

Without another word he turns away from them, goes to the door, and walks right into that shimmering light. There's no spark or crackle and certainly no explosion. One moment Bennewitz is there, the next he's not.

"You next," Walter says.

"Is it safe?" Turn asks, though knowing the question is a dumb one right after it leaves his mouth.

"Compared to being atomized to nothing – which is what we'll be in another ninety seconds if we stand here – then yes, I'd say she's safe."

Turn bites his lip. That was *not* the answer he wanted to hear.

"Listen," Walter continues, putting his hand on Turn's back and pushing him forward a bit, "I've done this nearly a dozen times now, and each time it's the same – a slight tingling, the feeling that my hair's full of static electricity, and then just like that, I'm there."

Turn looks back to see Walter's face. "Where's *there?*"

"Why don't you see for yourself," Walter says, and his pushing turns to a shove. Before Turn has time to react, he's entering the shimmering doorway…and then he's gone.

PART II
3 – WINDING DOWN

Blue Lake
Friday, May 25, 1979
4:05 AM

A total of 15 men sat in folding chairs in a non-descript hangar on a base in the middle of the Colorado Plateau. They were in the Four Corners region of New Mexico, and their eyes dart this way and that, hands shaking with adrenaline and trigger fingers twitching. They were in the same hangar on the edge of the base's airstrip that they had been just 4 hours before. *Was it just that long ago,* Ellis thinks as he looks out at them, *just 4 hours since I was lecturing them on what's to come?* The Dutchman chuckles to himself. *My God I was naïve!*

"Sir?" Chargin' Charlie says, catching the Dutchman's strange expression.

"Yes," Ellis says, clapping his hands together and coming out of his reverie, "let's get started."

"*Started?*" Bobbie scoffs from his spot in one of the back rows of men. "Hell, why don't we finish – I dunno about you, sir, but I've been up for damn-near 24 hours!"

There were grumblings of agreement to Bobbie's words, and Ellis puts his hands up to settle things.

"Alright, alright…" he says, waiting for the men to quiet back down, "…I'll keep this as short as I can."

As he says the words his eyes dart to the door in the back. General Anderholt is there, just coming into the room. He sees Ellis, nods, and leans up against the back wall, crossing his arms to listen. A few of the Blue Lake base guards are with him, and Ellis figures the general must have rushed here just as fast as he could. He ignores him for now, and puts his focus back on the men.

"CAT-1 and CAT-2 breached the lower levels, and CAT-1 even got into the Hall of Horrors and Nightmare Hall." Ellis looks to the men that were on those teams. "You men did a helluva lot of damage down there, and you saved a helluva lot of prisoners as well."

"Lost a helluva lot o' my friends too," John says, and the grumblings of agreement are louder than they were for Bobbie.

"CAT-3 up top was no different," Ellis continues, looking at John as he says the words. "Up there they turned off the sonic, breached the main HUB doors and made it to Level 2 before being forced back when the call to pullout was given."

"Helluva call," Aaron says with disgust, but Ellis ignores this as he scans his clipboard and starts reading off the dead.

"CAT-1 lost Sammy and Tommy while CAT-2 lost Walter, its leader."

"Said he was goin' back up to save as many more as he could," Emil says with a shrug, "but then we never saw him again."

"Had no choice but to hop on the last train when the call to leave came through," Jake adds.

Ellis nods and continues on with the death toll. "CAT-3 – which was the largest, broken down into two groups – lost Jerry, Paul, Johnny, Lewie, and Turn. And finally, CAT-4 lost Robbie."

"Now I'm the only super soldier left," Bobbie says with a shrug.

"We'll need your ability to withstand the Grays' mind attacks," Carl says from the side of the room. "You know they're not just going to let this attack go unpunished."

"We'll handle that when it comes," Ellis says. "Now in total that's 10 men in all, out of 25." He shakes his head. "40% casualty rate - terrible, *just terrible*!"

"But we destroyed the base," Mark says after a brief lull comes, "or at least killed everything down to the microbial level that was inside the hell hole." He looks back at the others as he says it, pumping his fist into the air a bit. "We sent that CED so far down the levels that there's nothing left, and won't be for some time."

"Forever, hopefully," Stan says from the back of the room, where all the MAT team members are.

"I couldn't agree more," Mark says, giving him a nod.

"That's three of us," Ellis says, "and from the looks on some of your faces, I'd say many of you men feel…"

Ellis trails off as the men before him narrow their eyes, then begin shaking their heads before hanging them. Ellis turns around to see what they're looking at, and his face takes on the same shocked and then saddened expression. There behind them, being wheeled in through the main hangar door by the base's guards, are the dead from the attack on Dulce…at least those that still had bodies to retrieve. The men watch silently for a moment, then as if thinking on the same wavelength, stand up and salute. Flag-draped coffins roll past, and in some cases, just a small cart with a flag on it and nothing else. Those, the men know, are all that indicates that Paul and Lewie had lived and were killed by the alien flashguns. After the bodies go by the men sit back down. The room is silent, until Moses speaks.

"Don't seem like much of a success."

"It was a success," Mark says.

"You're damn right it was a success," Ellis says, giving Moses a hard look until he nods as well, admitting the fact. Ellis frowns then, puts his hands on his hips and looks down at the hangar floor. "That's not to say it wasn't a *costly* success." He looks up to see many of the men nodding, or looking down. Either way, he knows they know what he's about to get at. "We lost Jerry and Paul and Lewie and Johnny…damn near the whole CAT-3 team that went in there. Besides that we lost all the others." Ellis shakes his head. "Costly indeed."

"But the base has been destroyed now, right?" David asks.

Stu steps forward to take that one. "We saw it with our own eyes as we got the hell out of there – Dulce Base blowing sky high…that upper level at least."

"And the lower levels?" Mark asks.

"Gone too," Stu says. "With a CED device, there *is* nothing left. Any aliens still there are gone, as are the humans that might have been captive."

"Could the Grays come back?" Ellis asks.

"They could," Stu says, "but there'd be nothing there for them. They'd have to rebuild everything, and the corporate structure isn't going to sign-off on that, not after what happened at the base in '75."

"So now what?" Moses says after a brief lull in which Stu steps back to lean against the wall.

"Yeah, is this it for our team then?" Aaron says.

"Or what's left of it," Bobbie adds.

"If you mean, 'are we disbanding you?'" Ellis says, "then the answer is 'no'."

"Might as well be disbanded," Aaron says. He sat toward the back of the room, his hands folded before him on the table, veins popping out of those muscled forearms. "Like you said, we've lost ten souls down there…and we're not even sure all of 'em are dead." He held up a hand before Mark could get a word in. "I know, I know…Stu's bomb-thingy blew everything up top and down bottom to kingdom come." He glanced around, narrowing his eyes suspiciously. "Yeah, *right*. We'd like to *think* that's what happened – and I for one would like to believe it, too – but the truth of the matter is that we just don't know." He glanced down at his watch. "It's been 4 hours since we got the hell out of there, the base 'blowing up' behind us" – he made that last comment with some quotation mark gestures in the air – "and in that time we don't know what's been happening."

"He's right," Carl speaks up, drawing everyone's eyes to him, for the words that were being spoken were hard-hitting, and the conversation had the men's undivided attention, "we don't know what's going on. For all we know, those lower levels could have just been *damaged*, not destroyed. For all we know, those tube trains are still running, the Grays are retaking the place, or at the very least, getting everything out of there that's of any value to them…including whatever was in those lower-level holding tanks, *and* any men we may have inadvertently left behind."

"*Shit*!" John scoffs. "And here I thought we were celebrating one *helluva* success. The more we babble on about it though, the more it sounds like we should never have tried in the first place."

"No one's saying that," Ellis says quickly.

"Then what *are* we saying?" Chargin' Charlie says, his eyes darting around to the men in the room, none of whom are eager to answer that one.

"All I'm saying," Aaron says after a few moments, "is that we need to be careful, *especially* about our expectations. The situation could be *wildly* different than we imagine, and now's not the time to lower our guard."

Donlon laughs. "You almost make it sound like there are Grays among us here and now!"

Aaron only cocks his head to that in a half-sort of shrug. Ellis narrows his eyes at the gesture, but in doing so the sleeplessness that he's managed to keep at bay comes surging back. He nearly swoons and has to blink a few times to get his bearings.

"Okay there, boss?" Emil speaks up, giving Ellis a sideways look. Ellis looks at him, and notices others looking at him strangely as well.

"Yeah…yeah," he says, "just tired is all."

"Shit, guess I'm not the only one that hasn't slept in 24 hours!" Bobbie says with a laugh, elbowing David beside him, who only frowns.

Carl steps forward then. "You men deserve a rest – you've earned it." He turns to the Dutchman. "That goes for you too, Ellis. Can't have you falling down dead on us now!"

Ellis gives an uneasy smile to that, and nods as Carl claps him on the back. The men in the room begin to get up and then filter out, most heading to the barracks for sleep, a couple hard-cores hitting up the mess hall for some chow first, maybe a workout.

"I'll turn-in in an hour or so," Ellis says to Carl as he starts for the door as well. "First I want to question a few of those female escapees."

"Be my guest," Carl says with a shrug, and then watches Ellis walk out.

4 – LEAKS

Ellis gets out into the hallway and is glad to see his son standing there. Mark is talking with some of the men that he'd fought with, but at the sight of his father he says his goodbyes and the group breaks up, the other men heading to the barracks. Ellis nods as he approaches.

"Lookin' a little tired there, dad," Mark says, narrowing his eyes a bit but flashing a smile as well. Ellis forgot how bright and vibrant that smile was. It'd been ten years since he'd seen it, ever since Mark had gone off-world with the Sirians.

"Feelin' a little tired too," Ellis replies, giving a half-hearted smile.

"I bet," Mark says with a laugh. "With the mission and the planning, I bet you're pushing *more* than 24 hours."

Ellis only frowns to that, then reaches out and grabs his son's arm. "We need to talk," he says, glancing this way and that to make sure no one's close enough to listen.

"What is it?" Mark says, alarm in his voice.

"Well, first of all…" Ellis says, glancing around one more time, then satisfied that no one is there, he focuses in on his son, "…what was with that Sirian ship back there at Dulce?"

Mark sighs. "Long story. What do you know of the off-world political situation as it currently stands?"

"Well," Ellis begins, "we know most of the treaties between the humans and the Grays have been broken, the same with the treaties between us and the lizards. But then we've known that since '75, just as we've known of the Grays' expansion into the various underground bases that used to be solely our own."

"And what of the disturbance in relations this has caused?"

Ellis shakes his head. "We know nothing of that."

Mark nods. "The Grays took advantage of the chaos created from the events in '75 to invade and conquer several of the older underground colonies. Apparently this has led to quite the fight in the Ashtar Collective, with many of the humanoids and the hybrids splitting off to join the Andro-Pleiadean Federation."

"That drastic?" Ellis says.

"It gets worse," Mark replies. "Ego is now being compressed in on itself. It's imploding on itself, and we're finding *huge* pockets of incredible negativity, not only here, but in other parts of the galaxy as well. On Sirius B, for instance, there's a terrible civil war going on right now. In Perseus, there are *21* systems getting ready to go to war in a battle between the Orion Group and the benevolent races of the Andromedan Council."

"Damn, how'd things get so dicey?"

Mark shakes his head and lets out a sigh. "Something in the universe is speeding up, dad…but we don't know what it is, where it is, or how to stop it."

"*God?*" Ellis asks, and Mark shrugs, saying, "Could be."

Silence falls for a moment as both men think on that, then Ellis speaks again.

"They're still focused on non-intervention, right?"

Mark nods again. "Nothing to worry about there. It's the Reptilians and some heartless humanoids that've joined them that we need to worry about. Together they've joined the interventionists of the Draco-Orion Empire."

"*Great,*" Ellis says with a sigh and a long eye roll.

"There's more," Mark continues. "The Sirius-B system – aside from Arcturus and our own Sol group – has been shaken badly by this split between the two opposing Ashtarian factions. The division we see on Earth because of events in '75 has expanded well beyond the stars. The Pleiadean-backed Sirian humanoids and the Orion-backed Sirian Reptilians have never been at each other's throat as much as they are now."

"You make it sound like what happened at Dulce four years ago is just the tip of the iceberg."

"It is. What happened down in that base caused a chain reaction that's rippled across this whole sector of the galaxy. Before '75, the Reptilians had been invited to the peace talks in Telos, an act of good faith, sure, but a clear signal as well that the humanoids wanted to put the past behind them, and move forward in a peaceful and productive way."

Ellis scoffs. "It's that peace that might've scared the damn lizards more than anything."

"Many were saying that the invitation to the peace talks was nothing more than a gesture," Mark says with a shrug, "and one the Reptilians-Gray alliance would *never* have attended anyways. Most figured that their insatiable appetite for conquest and empire-building would make whatever peace treaties they signed nothing more than promises waiting to be broken."

"Which is what they've become."

Mark nods. "And now the conflicts in Sirius between the Andro-Pleiadean-backed Ashtar forces and the Draco-Orion-backed Ashtar forces - which were infiltrated and commandeered by Draco-Orion agents - have now spread to the Sol system, as both stellar superpowers have focused on this most strategic system, intent on protecting their respective 'interests' here from being subverted by the other side."

"Not sure I could understand it all if I wanted to," Ellis says with a chuckle, one that makes him realize how tired he is.

"You should get some rest, dad." Mark can see how tired his father is. *He's 65*, he thinks, *at that age he should be down in Florida, sleeping late and enjoying the golf course as much as he can.*

"I will," Ellis replies, "but first, let me get at what I think might be a bigger problem for us…at least for the moment."

"*Oh?*"

"I think we have some traitors in our midst." Ellis narrows his eyes, but says nothing, waiting for his father to go on. Ellis does so. "I'm not sure who's all involved, but I think it might go all the way up to MJ12. I think it might even involve elements of Delta Force, the Black Berets, Air Force Blue Berets, the Secret Service, FBI Division Five, CIA stormtroopers *and* Dulce Base security."

"Damn," Mark says after giving out a surprised whistle.

"A few years back several of our best scientists were captured by the Grays after they had discovered the 'Grand Deception,' as we called it. It involved the permanent abduction of thousands of humans to Dulce and other bases for God only knows what purposes." He looks sternly at his son. "I don't have to tell you that it's a clear violation of *all* the existing treaties."

"You sure it's a conspiracy?"

"I don't believe for one second that MJ12 was unaware of these abductees. What *I* think happened is that those above MJ12 – the Black Monk/Majic agency – *was* aware and had agreed to an exchange in human lives for advanced alien technology."

"So someone in MJ12 is against us…but what about someone here at Blue Lake?"

Ellis nods. "You heard me mention Delta Force just now. Well, who heads them up?"

"On our team?" Mark asks. "Aaron Haney. Overall…well, wouldn't that be…" his eyes widen when the realization hits him, "…General Anderholt?" Mark scoffs. "You don't think he's mixed up in all this, do you, dad?"

"I don't know what to think anymore," Ellis says. He shakes his head, sighs, and rolls his eyes. To Mark, he's clearly blaming himself. "Look, I didn't know about it until after we started the attack,"

"But *how* did you know?"

"Simple," Ellis says, looking back at his son, "though I didn't notice it at the time." He shakes his head and looks down at the ground again before looking back up at Mark. "It was the tube trains! There's no way that last train of women could have gone on its own unless someone on the outside made it so. That someone would have to be high-ranking, and with access to the area bases."

"Oh, c'mon!" Mark says. "That could have been the Grays in another base."

"Sending their captives to safety?" Ellis asks with a narrow-eyed look.

"Oh, Jeez! I mean…what are you saying?" Mark says, his face screwing up in concern. "Are you telling me that we've got a traitor in our midst?"

"That's *exactly* what I'm telling you."

It was Mark shaking his head and rolling his eyes and letting out a sigh this time. "God*damn* it!" he says, slamming one fist down into his open palm. "The Sirians warned me about something like this when I was there. They said, 'trust no one, even those that you *think* are on your team.'" He shakes his head and scoffs before looking back at his father. "The way I took it at the time, they were telling me not to trust *you*, dad." He shakes his head again. "I just couldn't believe what they were saying, and it was a big reason I decided to leave and come back to Earth." He sighs again. "Now I know it *wasn't* you they were talking about, but this…this…*someone* that's playing both sides."

"Playing both sides is right," Ellis says, "and I have no doubt that the debriefing we just did will somehow filter back to the Grays." He shakes his head again, swears silently under his breath. "*Everything* we do, *everything* we say – the Grays will find out."

"Until we find this traitor in our midst," Mark says, and Ellis nods.

"And until then, we need…"

Ellis trails off as Eddie comes into view, a smile on his face and his eyes locked on the both of them. The Japanese-American is no doubt still in a good mood from the joyride he took on the small alien fighter craft he pilfered from Dulce Base.

"Mark…just the man I've been lookin' for," he says when he's a dozen feet from them.

Mark turns around. "Oh, Eddie…well, yeah…what is it?"

"Stan's got a question about the X-22." Eddie gave a half-shrug, half-wince. "Says he might have to scrap the whole damn thing if you don't get your ass down to Hangar 7 right away and tell him what's what…" Eddie puts his hands up at Mark's expression. "Hey, his words not mine!"

Mark rolls his eyes before looking back to his father.

"It's alright – catch up to me later," Ellis says, and he starts down the hallway again. "I'll be with the women."

5 – HEATHER

Blue Lake
Friday, May 25, 1979
5:25 AM

The Dutchman keeps replaying the words his son had said as he walks down one of the lower-level hallways of the Blue Lake base. *Trust no one, even those that you* think *are on your team.*

Ellis didn't like it. He'd never known the Sirians or the Nordics to worry easily, either for themselves or for others. They were analytical, higher-level beings that put logic foremost and emotion much further down the list…if it was even on there at all. Ellis hadn't been face to face with one of the beings in years – not since the Lake Oswego Incident – but he doubted they'd changed much in that time. And what Mark was saying was true – with the treaties nearly in tatters and the Grays and Reptilians pounding the drums of war once again, anything could happen. Earth *could* become the galactic battlefield that many always said it would, though Ellis couldn't quite make himself believe things were that bad.

"Yet," he says under his breath, and just before he reaches the area he'd been heading to, a row of nondescript and unmarked doors. He goes past two more and then stops at the third. He gives a polite, two-rap knock and then turns the knob.

"Hello, hello," he says amiably upon entering, trying to inject some cheer into what he knows is about the un-cheeriest situation one could imagine. *He* can barely imagine it, being held in a cage, or a vat, or God forbid, worse. Yet these women had not only done that, they'd survived it.

The room was large, about the size of an elementary school gym, and several men in lab coats were going around with clipboards, talking to the women they could. There were around a hundred women there, most in hospital gowns but a few still halfway naked, with hundreds more in similar areas around the base. Many were crying, though most seemed to be taking it stoically, looking forward with the kind of thousand-yard stares that Ellis remembers from his days in WWII. He can only imagine what has brought on those looks. The endless experiments, the sleep deprivation, the forced sex, the impregnations…it was all too much. There'd of course be abortions, dissections, implants, surgical removals, and even complete mind-wipes. The way some of the women leaned their heads against the wall, a thin stream of drool coming from the corner of their mouths, made Ellis think that mind-wipes had indeed been employed. He gritted his teeth and tried to hate the Grays even more, if that was at all possible.

Women in nursing uniforms were also moving around, giving injections, taking temperatures and measuring blood pressure. They too jotted notes down on clipboards, though Ellis knew it was the men that were getting the real information. Much of it didn't even need to come from talking – the way the women looked, certain marks on them…it all told a tale. That tale was one of a battle between two races – the humans and the Grays – and as Ellis looks at that room of more than a hundred women, he's not sure who's winning.

"Ellis!" a muffled shout comes, and the Dutchman looks over to see Stu there in a white lab coat, clipboard in hand, and his other hand waving him over. Ellis nods and starts that way.

"Stu," he says when he's a few feet away, and Stu nods before turning back to the woman sitting on an exam table in front of him.

"This is Heather…a *very* interesting abductee."

Ellis offers a smile and sticks out his hand. "Hello, Heather."

"Sir," she says, keeping her eyes mostly directed at the floor.

"Heather here was in captivity for nearly a year, and during that time she saw a lot, suffered a lot too."

"Oh?" Ellis says, glancing from Heather to Stu and back again.

"You can say that again," Heather says after a moment of silence has passed.

"But I'd rather hear you say it," Ellis says.

Heather frowns, but then launches into it. "I was taken at night, from my home in Texas, the classic abductee story about waking up, seeing Grays at the foot of the bed, and then suddenly being aboard their ship." She rolls her eyes. "It was the operating room, of course."

"Why 'of course'?" Stu asks.

Heather scoffs. "Why, because I'm a woman, that's why! As soon as they get a woman they shoot someone's – or some*thing's* – sperm into her and boom, just like that she's pregnant."

"And that happened to you?" Ellis asks.

"Three times."

"*Three*…" Stu starts, but trails-off.

"Three times," Heather repeats. "They impregnate us and then about three months later they come and harvest the fetus, taking it out of us and then…I dunno, off to some lab somewhere, I guess."

"And this happens to all the women that wind up in Dulce?" Ellis asks.

"All but the ones they mutate into something else." She glances around and then lowers her voice. "Did you see the tanks?"

Both men nod, but Ellis is the one to speak. "Lots of women in those tanks, lots of women that look like you."

"He means, 'beautiful' women," Stu says, and Heather blushes for a moment before an awkward silence falls.

Ellis takes on an amused smile. "And I guess you're about what they're looking for, then…huh?" Heather looks up at him as if she doesn't know what he's talking about, so he fumbles forward, nearly tripping over his words. "I mean…uh…they want petite women in their early twenties – *maybe* early thirties – am I even halfway right?"

Heather laughs. "I'd say you about hit the nail on the head there, sir."

"But there was more than just women down there," Stu says, and Heather nods as she collects herself.

"They like small to medium size men in their mid-twenties to mid-forties. Their favorites, however, are dark-haired boys between five to nine. The boys are favored because at that age their bodies are rapidly growing, and their atomic material is adaptable in the transfer chamber."

"*Transfer chamber?*" Ellis says.

Heather shakes her head and looks down at the ground. "I'm not sure what it is exactly, just that it strips the flesh from the bones and the soul from the body…or something like that."

"*God!*" Stu says.

"Anything else?" Ellis asks after a few moments of silence have passed. "*Anything.*"

Heather cocks her head to one side, as if trying to shake out any remaining memories that might be stubbornly clinging to her mind.

"The young women are usually small in size and frequently *very* fertile. The men are used for sperm, that's it. I have no idea why they prefer small to average size men."

"Might be for control purposes," Stu says.

"Might be," Heather continues. "I only mention the most common people you'll find down there are the small, young men and the petite women." She shakes her head and stares at Ellis. "But, let me stress that there are *all types* of people being held against their will in that base! There are tall, heavy men and women that are big too. There are, teenagers, elderly folks and *very* young girls in those cages…grade school kids." She frowns and shakes her head. "They're in the vats, too."

After that last Heather buries her head in her hands and starts to cry. Ellis looks at Stu guiltily, as if he were the cause of this, while Stu just rushes forward to put his hands on Heather's shoulders to comfort her.

"I'm…sorry," Heather says through her tears, trying to look up at Ellis and Stu again.

"No, no!" both men say at the same time, their hands out in front of them in placating gestures. It doesn't work and the tears continue. Ellis finally finishes with a, "Maybe we should–"

"Heather!"

The shout comes from behind them, and both Ellis and Stu turn.

"Mark!" Heather shouts out from behind them, and just as both men's eyes focus on Ellis's son. Neither are able to say anything, for Heather jumps from the exam table and nearly knocks them over as she begins rushing across the room.

"Oh, Heather!" Mark says when the two of them meet in the middle of the room and embrace. They look into each other's eyes, and Mark begins to wipe away her tears. "I never thought I'd see you again," he says. "Thank God I was wrong!"

Heather just looks up at him, smiling, with a fresh round of tears coming…though tears of happiness this time.

"Um…" Stu says, looking from Ellis to Mark and back again, while Ellis gives an audible clearing of his throat. Neither Mark nor Heather look over at them.

"Do you two *know* each other?" Ellis asks a moment later. That finally elicits a response from Mark.

"Yeah, dad, we do. And I'll tell you what, I think we'll be leaving." He says that last looking from Heather to his father. "It's been a long day – for all of us – but for the abductees like Heather here the most. She needs rest, and I'll walk her back to her room and make sure she gets it."

Both men nod to that, though Mark doesn't notice. He's already helping Heather to her feet, his arm around her shoulders and a concerned look on his face. He gives a nod to both men as he passes them, then gets the door open. A moment later they're out in the hallway and Ellis and Stu are alone once again.

6 – ABDUCTIONS

Ellis watches them go. When they're gone, however, he stops forcing himself to smile and lets his frown come out. He lets out a sigh and shakes his head while putting hands on his hips. He's just about to say what's on his mind when he happens to glance up. The expression on Stu's face stops all thoughts cold.

"What are you lookin' at me like that for, Stu?" he says with a laugh, though a nervous one at that.

Stu immediately straightens up and looks away, stopping the intent staring he was giving Ellis's way. "Uh…it's nothing. Nothing! Just had my mind wander off there for a sec."

Ellis narrows his eyes at Stu, as if he's not sure he's getting the full story. For his part, Stu just hopes what he was told in his room after the debriefing isn't true. If it is, well…he knows this could very well be the last time he talks to Ellis.

"Been a long night, I know," Ellis says a moment later, then focuses back on the matter at hand. "How much of what she says is true?"

"Heather?" Stu says, relieved that Ellis has changed the subject. "From what we're getting or from the other reports?" Stu asks the question then scoffs. "Why, *all* of it!"

"*All of it?*" Ellis says, turning to look back at him with his face screwed up in disbelief.

Stu nods. "Over 90% of the female abductees report being inseminated by aliens…and the other 10% probably were but can't remember."

"Are they trying to hybridize our species?"

"Yes," Stu says without pause. "They're breeding slave-warriors for the upcoming war with the other alien races."

"The Pleiadians?"

Stu nods again. "Them, as well as the Sirians. The Grays will have help from the serpentine races in orbit around Earth, Venus and Mars."

Ellis sighs, looking very much his 65 years. He glances around, sees the table that Heather was just sitting on, and gets up on it himself. He begins to slowly kick his feet back and forth as they hang down from the table and above the floor, much as a child would as they waited for the doctor to come and see them. *The only sucker that'll be seen at the end of* this *examination*, Ellis thought to himself, *will be me.*

"How could we have been so dumb," he says after a few moments of sitting there, his legs swaying.

Stu scoffs. "What's 'dumb,' exactly? Making what we thought was a good decision twenty-five years ago only to find out it was shit?" He scoffs again, shakes his head. "And much of what's taking place was set in stone *long* before Ike made that deal back in the 50s. Hell, remember what your own son said back at the briefing last night before we even went into Dulce?"

Mark narrows his eyes at Stu as if he's not quite sure, but says nothing.

"The first Gray motherships came over a three year period," Stu continues, using that near-photographic memory of his to recall *exactly* what Mark had said just hours before, "from 1787 to 1789…right as the French Revolution was getting underway. He talked of probe ships that they'd sent way back in *1645*." He scoffed again as he said that last, drawing Ellis's eyes. "Can you believe that? My *God*, 300 years ago! And they kept comin' – another mothership behind the sun in 1859 and then one behind Mars fifty years after that."

"Don't forget the one behind Pluto, either," Ellis says, "the one that looks like a moon."

"The moon we haven't discovered…*yet*."

Ellis looks up at Stu. "You know that Mark has spent a great deal of time off-world, and you know that he's served with the 177th."

Stu nods. "I know."

"Ellis, you know how I feel about time travel. If we can–"

Ellis holds up his hands, stopping Stu's words. "Stu, you know how I feel about this, and you know how General Anderholt feels about this."

Stu's face screws up in exasperation. "I know, but–"

"Stu," Ellis says sternly, and with a stern look, "I *don't* want to talk about it."

A silence falls in the small exam room, the conversation replaced with tension. It lasts several moments, awkwardness filling the space between the two men. It's finally broken by the door slamming open, Carl standing behind it.

"Ellis!" Carl shouts as he starts across the room.

"What is it?" Ellis says, getting off the exam table, alarm in his voice.

"Been lookin' all over for you – a report just came over the wire from Scoff Air Force Base in Illinois."

"General Herres," Ellis says without pause, and Carl nods. Ellis does too, saying, "Let's go."

Ellis takes three steps and then a deep rumbling sound fills the room. Stu and Carl both narrow their eyes and look at Ellis questioningly.

"Haven't eaten since before the mission," Ellis finally says, his face reddening a bit.

"Well Damn, Ellis," Carl laughs, "they just served chow thirty minutes ago!"

A smile creases up one corner of Ellis' mouth. "You buyin'?"

"*Shit!*" Carl says, and turns to the door, waving his arm in a following gesture, "c'mon."

~~~

The men walk down the long hallways of the Blue Lake base, looking into the small windows of the doors they pass. Many are the same kind of exam rooms they were just in, though most are larger. Women are inside, the women that Ellis and the others freed from Dulce. Men in lab coats are talking with them, jotting down notes on clipboards and occasionally nodding…without looking up, of course. It's all business here at Blue Lake, and that's the way General Anderholt likes it. Though often absent, he runs a tight ship – both men can see that plainly.
~~~

"So what's Herres saying?" Ellis asks as they walk, keeping his voice down and cutting himself off completely when they pass by others.

"It's about Black Knight. It's operational again."

"Well, it's always been operational. What's–"

"It's transmitting again," Carl says.

Ellis frowns and cocks his head. "Well, I'll be."

The men quiet down as they enter a particularly busy area of the base, one with more soldiers moving about. The mess hall and breakfast are up ahead, so Carl decides to steer the conversation back to what's going on around them, not up in orbit.

"Word is that the abduction process is entering a new phase," he says as they walk.

"Oh?" Ellis replies.

"We've heard chatter on it before, but now these new women are telling us that the aliens aren't so much interested in using them for pregnancies anymore.

"Then what *are* they interested in using them for?"

"As guides."

They reach the mess hall just as Carl finishes, and Ellis pauses there with his hand on the door, looking over at him. "*Guides?*" he says.

"Guides," Carl repeats, and puts his own hand on the door to push it open.

Inside the mess hall were a wide array of people – soldiers in uniform, most likely base guards; scientists in lab coats, probably the same that were questioning the women; civilians in civilian attire, office and personnel workers that were sworn to secrecy; and finally a few of the men that'd gone into Dulce…and made it out alive. Ellis waves to them as he and Carl heads for the food counter, and they wave back, smiling but probably thankful that their commander looks too busy to come and join them. Carl and Ellis get their food – meatloaf by the looks of it, with green beans and mashed potatoes on the side (*can't even serve breakfast, the bastards,* Ellis thinks) – and then heads to an empty table on the emptier side of the room. That coupled with all the voices in the room making a low hum and the two know that their chances of being overheard are slim to none.

"Seems the Grays are starting in on the second, maybe even the third, phase of their plans," Carl continues once they're seated and picking at their food. "Before it was just getting the abducted women pregnant, though of course they always took the babies before they could be born here on Earth."

"Sped up the 9-month process?" Ellis asks.

"Something like that, though usually the women would miss one or two periods here on Earth before being abducted again, whereupon the egg or developing fetus would be removed."

"And then they'd be sent on their way, none the wiser for it," Ellis says, and Carl nods.

"Now…what do you think happened to those half-alien, half-human babies…the hybrids?"

"I have a feeling you're about to tell me," Ellis says with a slight smile before scooping some mashed potatoes into his mouth.

"They're growing up, getting older…ready to get out into the world. And to do that, the Grays are now using abductees as guides, a kind of teacher for how the world works, if you will."

"I don't get you."

Carl leans back and takes in a deep breath. "Consider going to another planet. You don't know anyone or how anything works, even the most basic things, like that it gets dark at night and then light again in the morning, or that there are all kinds of animals and plants and insects, some benign, some not. The point is, Ellis, these hybrid alien-humans don't know *any of this*, so they need human guides to meet with them and tell them how things work. That's why the hybridization plan started, and why it's been going on for at least 10 years now, taking the embryo out after the third month to go the rest of the way in their laboratories. The hybrids need to replace the spiritually-based humans. The particular combination of the hybrid DNA doesn't allow for a soul, so humans can't reincarnate in hybrid bodies. When hybrids cover the earth and there are no more humans, there'll be no place for Earth-based humans to reincarnate. Eventually the hybrids will run things, but for now it's the Illuminati." He chuckles as he gets ready to shovel in another mouthful of green beans. "And hybrids don't need to eat that shit like the Grays do."

"Ugh, don't remind me – I'm eating here."

Carl smiles. "You know the Grays don't eat – they 'feed' off of human and animal vital fluids by rubbing that 'liquid protein' shit onto their bodies, which is then absorbed through the skin."

Ellis puts down the mouthful of mashed potatoes he'd been about to shovel into his mouth and gives Carl a hard look.

"But it's not just *feeding* off human and animal proteins and fluids, they also allegedly feed off the 'life energy,' the 'vital essence' or 'soul energy' of humans," Carl continues, not taking notice of Ellis or his discomfort at all. "Damn Reptilians do the same thing." He shakes his head, finally looking up at Ellis. "Makes me wanna puke."

"Yeah, me too," Ellis says, pushing his tray away and looking a little green in the face. *First not enough sleep, now my stomach feeling like shit,* he thinks.

"Anyways, the hybrids will do away with much of that need…at least for the need for so many Grays to be here on Earth doing all the work.

"But…*why?*"

"So the Grays can eventually take over." Carl shakes his hand as if clearing away his words. ""But let's be honest, here – the Grays aren't the real threat at all. Some Grays – the living ones, at least – are hybrids already, a mix of Reptilian and Sirian. Others are mostly robotic, though so advanced that we can't tell."

"*Take over?* Don't be absurd, Carl, there's–"

"It's happening already," Carl interrupts, "and closer to us than you might even realize. For instance, I doubt any of these hybrids are in positions of power – *yet* – but what of the people that are *guiding* them?"

"You think they're in the government?"

"And the military," Carl says quickly.

Ellis leans back this time, sighing as he does so. "I have to tell you, Carl – and this is just between you and me – but I've been getting a sneaking suspicion lately that Aaron isn't exactly…on our side."

"You've been getting that too, eh?"

"Wait, you've…"

Ellis trails-off as Carl nods. "First noticed it on some reports I got about missions he did in South America."

"Mark says that last night he got a bit jumpy when questioned about Johnny, Andy and Turn's deaths."

Carl frowns to that. "It's probably nothing. Who really troubles me, though, is Donlon."

"Colonel Roger Donlon?" Ellis says, and a little too loudly in his surprise. He quiets down. "He's about as strait-arrow as they come."

"Not if what I'm reading in the Herres report is true," Carl says as he takes a bit of his green beans. "From what we're getting off the telescopic reading analyzers…well, I thing he might be working with the Grays."

"Carl, that's absurd," Ellis says, leaning in to look in his friend's eyes. "You got some proof on this?"

"It's all in the reports, which I'll show you right after we finish up here. Suffice it to say, he's been–"

"Sir."

Both men turn about to see a young soldier standing there and looking at Ellis.

"Sir," the soldier continues, "General Herres at Kirtland's on the phone for you."

Ellis nods and turns back to Carl. "Better not keep the old man waiting."

"What, you're not gonna finish that?" Carl says, glancing from Ellis to the tray and back again.

"Be my guest," Ellis says with a scoff, and begins to follow the soldier out of the mess hall.

7 – REUNION

Blue Lake
Friday, May 25, 1979
6:18 AM

Mark keeps his arm around Heather's shoulders and that concerned look on his face as the two walk away from the door to the examination room and down the hallway. They hadn't gone more than a dozen feet when Mark stops, looks over his shoulder, then pushes Heather up against the wall. He looks into her eyes deeply for a moment, then dives in for a kiss. It's returned, with vigor.

"Oh, Mark," Heather says when they're done, "I was worried I'd never *see* you again!"

"Then why'd you volunteer to–"

"I'm not talking about that," Heather replies quickly, cutting off Mark's words, "I'm talking about you being off-world so long, and then all those years you spent with the 177th?" She trails-off and looks away, shaking her head and appearing on the verge of tears. Finally she looks back. "Mark, what if something had happened, what if–"

"But it didn't, and it *won't*," Mark says, pulling her in for a hug.

"It's just that…"

Heather trails-off as she hears the sound of footsteps coming down the hallway. She and Mark take a step back from one another, smooth down their clothes, and try to look as though nothing much is happening. A moment later Eddie and Stan appear, both talking about the alien fighter craft that Eddie pilfered from Dulce. As they near the two they nod, never breaking their conversation, and then vanish down the hallway as it turns a corner past that set of exam rooms.

"Maybe there's somewhere else we can talk," Heather says once they're gone.

Mark nods. "This way."

~~~

Thirty minutes later the two of them are lying in Mark's bed, both sweaty from their bout of lovemaking. Heather rolls over on her side and looks at Mark staring up at the ceiling of the small, hotel-room-like officer's quarters.

"What was it like?" she asks.

"What was what like?"

"Time travel…going into the future…*all* of it."

Mark sighs. "Not as glamorous as you might think. For one, it's hell on the body and the mind. The 177th might have zapped me into the future for 10 years and then zapped me right back to the moment I left, but that doesn't mean I haven't aged those 10 years both in body and mind."

"And spirit?" Heather asks, looking over at him.

Mark cocks his head to one side in a sort of shrug. "I suppose so. After what I've seen and done…well, I suppose so."

Heather rolls over onto her stomach, the better to stare into Mark's face. "And what *did* you see…and are they still fighting in 2036?"

Mark nods. "Still fighting in 2036 and probably will be for years." He scoffs. "We keep fucking it up so much that we *have* to keep going back in and redoing it, over and over."

"And the Grays aren't getting wise to that?"

"Oh, they are…and that's probably why we keep losing." He sighs again. "I can't even *begin* to tell you how many men we've lost, *good* men too, the kind that don't come around more than once a century."

"How far back are you having to go to find them?"

Mark chuckles. "Commander Titor had just pulled six of 'em out of the Spanish-American War when I left. My God, Heather, they're
~~~

from 1898…damn-near one hundred years ago!"

"Can they even use our modern weapons…not to mention the futuristic stuff?"

"Titor's solved that with the computer-mind uploads. Most become masters of both 20th-century and 21st-century armaments *real* quick…and probably know more than most of the men on this base here."

Heather sighs and rolls back over to look up at the ceiling. "Just seems strange is all…constantly fighting in the same year, having to recruit further and further back in time…when will it all just end?"

"It has to some day," Mark says, rolling over onto his side now to look at her. "Now, why don't we talk about you for awhile? Tell me…what was it like down there?"

"Oh God," Heather says, rolling her eyes, "I wouldn't know where to begin."

"How about with your abduction? You know I was against that right from the get-go."

Heather scoffs. "Then you shouldn't spend so much time off-world or in different times – you'd be here instead, able to tell me what to do."

"Heather, I didn't mean it like that, I–"

"What's there to say anyways?" Heather says quickly, cutting off his words. "We went with the planned abduction, going with a group of women. It went well, we were taken onto a large ship of some sort – perhaps a mothership – and then taken to Dulce. It happened fast, getting put down on the lower levels, and after that they started picking us off one by one, either impregnating us, tinkering with our DNA, or cutting us up and using us as food."

"Even the women?"

"Even the women," Heather confirms. "It's not like it was just a couple years ago, Mark. It's like the Grays don't have as much use for the women as they once did. Before they'd *never* allow one to be used for food, but now, well…"

"They're moving on to the next phase of their plan," Mark says.

"And we need to be moving on to ours," Heather replies, and she rolls over and off the bed. Mark stares at her beautiful and naked body for a moment before she begins picking up her clothes and putting them back on.

"And what might that be?" Mark says as he too rolls off the bed and begins retrieving his clothes. Watching Heather there in the act of dressing, however, makes him wonder why he's doing so.

"Well, it's complicated but we know that…*hey*, you letch!"

"What?" Mark laughs as he gets his arms around Heather's body again, begins to unfasten the bra she'd just put on. "I've been in space for a *long* time, haven't felt your body in even longer."

"We have to–"

"See to your every need and desire," Mark says as he begins kissing the back of her neck.

That does it – Heather gives up her protestations and turns about, kisses Mark full on the mouth. Within moments they're back on the bed, their clothes once again piled on the floor about them.

~~~

Around the same time that Heather and Mark are getting back into it, Stu is leaving the mess hall. One thought is on his mind – *who the hell can I trust…and will they believe me?*

He gets the answer right away when Captain Moses Cochrane comes around a corner in the hallway. Stu recognizes him right away as one that'd gone into Dulce, though in more of a support position as a helicopter pilot. Still…*he knows*, Stu thinks, and as the two pass by each other he reaches out his hand and grabs hold of Moses' arm. Moses gives him a sharp look and is about to offer a rebuke as well, but Stu says what he has to say first.

"Moses," he says, looking up into the pilot's eyes, "for the love of God, remember that Aaron gets back just after midnight."

"*What?"* Moses says, his face screwing up in a look of confusion and bewilderment.

But Stu is already walking down the hallway, hoping his few words will prove enough.
~~~

8 – IN TOO DEEP

Blue Lake
Friday, May 25, 1979
6:49 AM

Back in his room, Ellis can't stop thinking about what Carl had said about Donlon. The Dutchman simply couldn't believe it – *Donlon's no traitor, I'm* sure *of it!*

But was he? That thought kept coming back to him over and over…what was he sure of anymore? Mark had spoken of Aaron, but Carl assured him that was nothing…despite whatever it was that'd happened down in South America. And then there was the Black Knight Satellite. *How the hell'd it get started again?*

It's all too much, and Anderholt wasn't able to clear any of it up – he'd never even *heard* of this report from Herres. "What the hell's that old bird doin' in on this?" he'd said when Ellis had brought up the subject. "He reports to Jones in the Pentagon and that's it – takes orders and passes 'em on, nothing more than a middle man."

So now Ellis was thinking of that too, and wondering if Carl will have him up by dinner, and then he can look at that report that–

Ellis stops dead in his tracks. There on his bed is a plain white folder, "Lab Samples' marked across it in red letters. 'Lab Samples' was always used because it was less likely to draw prying eyes than 'Top Secret;' people figured if they opened it, they'd get the plague. Ellis knew the truth – folders marked with that label contained highly classified material, almost always dealing with the secret space program, the humans serving off-world, and of course the latest alien political and economic intelligence reports. Ellis had seen many of those folders, but he hadn't seen one in nearly a year, and he'd *never* seen one outside a highly restricted office or archive setting. *What was it doing here?*

Ellis moves over and picks it up, his need for sleep and the sick feeling in his stomach from lunch both forgotten. He sits at the small table in his room and opens the folder, flips through the pages.

It all comes out. The real reason for the attack on Dulce, the sham SALT-II talks that President Carter was involved in, and even Illuminati and Rothschild family plans for speeding up the collapse of the economy while furthering the expansion of a vast secret military complex under the Denver International Airport. And then the real bomb hits. There on Page 9 was an image of Carl, the same Carl that Ellis had been eating lunch with just a short time before. He begins to read, and his eyes go wide.

KNOCK, KNOCK!

The short, sharp raps of two knocks come at the door, and Ellis's attention is torn from the pages. He closes the folder and looks to the door, tensing up as he does so. For a moment he thinks, *say nothing, let them think you're asleep*, but then his sense of duty takes over and he calls out, "Yes?"

"Ellis, it's me."

Carl, Ellis thinks and he slides the folder under a small stack of magazines, *TIME* and *LIFE* mostly, but a few *Popular Mechanics*. Then he goes to the door. He stands there for a moment, wondering what to do. Then he opens it.

"I've got that report," Carl says, holding up a manila envelope, "the one mentioning Donlon. Thought the way your mind is racin' you might like to see it, you know, before you hit the hay."

He nods at Ellis's bed as he says that last, and Ellis nods back. "Yes, yes…I do, come in…have a seat."

Carl comes in, handing over the envelope as he does so. "Pretty dry stuff that ol' Herres is sendin' our way," he says as he closes the door behind him, and – making sure Ellis isn't watching – locks it too. Then he moves into the room to give Ellis some space.

"Usually is," Ellis says as he flips over the top cover of the envelope and begins scanning the pages inside. For the most part it looks to be diagrams of bases, and looking at their names, Ellis quickly determines that each has a tube station beneath it. He continues to flip the pages, scanning headlines and passing over numbers. He's just about to ask Carl what he thinks when his friend speaks up instead.

"Hey!" Carl shouts out, and Ellis tenses up, turns back to look at him. "Did you read the article about high speed photometers in this February issue of *Popular Mechanics*?" he asks, reaching for the magazine. Ellis's heart skips a beat, but he can't make himself call out. "Here, let me show you…*hey*, what's this." As Carl begins to turn back around, Ellis doesn't need to look to know what'll be in his friend's hand. He does anyway, and sees the white folder marked 'Lab Results.'

"What's this?" Carl asks, looking from the folder to Ellis.

"It's nothing, Carl, just…"

Ellis trails-off as Carl puts the folder back down on the desk, slowly and with a sigh. After that he crosses his arms, looks down at the floor and begins to shake his head.

"Oh, Ellis, Ellis, Ellis…what ever are we gonna do with you?"

Ellis's eyes narrow in doubt and confusion, but he says nothing.

Carl looks back up at the Dutchman. "How long have you known, Ellis?"

"Known what?"

"*Everything*."

"I don't know what you're talking about, Carl, and you're starting to scare me. You–"

Carl begins to chuckle, and then laugh. "Oh, Ellis…*scare you?*" He laughs again. "We're not gonna scare you…we're gonna kill you."

Ellis's eyes narrow and his brow furrows. His heart begins to race and pump adrenaline into his system, and as the flight-or-flight response kicks in, Ellis wonders what he's gotten himself into, and how. Before he can get another question in, however, Carl is reaching into his pants pocket. Ellis's eyes go wide as his friend pulls out a flash gun.

"I'm sorry, Ellis," Carl says as he points the weapon at the Dutchman, "you were always a good friend to me."

Ellis puts his hands up in a 'wait' kind of gesture. "Carl, you don't have to–"

ZAP!

Carl pulls the trigger and the flash gun fires. The electric-like bolt that shoots out strikes Ellis and his eyes roll up into his head before he crumples to the floor.

"What the..." Carl says, looking down at the flash gun in his hand. He sees then that it's set on a lower setting than 'vaporize,' and understands why Ellis is still laying there and not a small pile of ash.

Probably better this way, he thinks, and moves forward. He steps over Ellis, grabs the white 'Lab Results' folder from the table, and then heads to the door. He pauses, gives a final look over his shoulder at the Dutchman lying there dead, then opens the door and goes back out into the hallway.

9 – BETRAYAL

Blue Lake
Friday, May 25, 1979
7:18 AM

Mark and Heather are still cuddling in bed when the door to their room bursts open. Blue Lake guards rush in, handguns drawn, and one even holding a machine gun.

"What…what are you doing!" Mark shouts out as the men begin to file into the room. Beside him Heather pulls the sheet up to cover herself. "What is this, Goddamn it, what–"

Before Mark can say another word, however, and before any answer to his query comes, one of the base soldiers comes forward, grabs him by the shoulder, and throws him back down to the bed. Before Mark can resist, he feels a knee dig into his back, one arm is grabbed and pulled behind him, and then the other.

"No!" Heather shouts beside him, and Mark turns his head to see a solder giving her the same treatment, the sheet now off of her and her breasts exposed.

"Damn you!" Mark shouts, but the knee digs into his back even more. A moment later he feels cold metal on his wrists and then hears the unmistakable sound of handcuffs clicking together. After that the knee comes off his back, the hand once again grabs his shoulder, and he's pulled over onto his back. He looks over at Heather and sees the soldier pull her up and begin marching her toward the door.

"Where are you taking her!" Mark shouts. "Will someone please tell me what the *hell* is going on here!"

He watches as the solder gets Heather out the door, she kicking and screaming all the while. There's still the soldier pinning him down, plus another three in the room with guns drawn and pointed his way. Mark is just about to start shouting out his questions again when Jake appears in the doorway. Mark wasn't on the same CAT team as the young major, but he recognizes him well enough from their pre-mission briefing.

"Jake!" he shouts. "Tell me what's going on. Tell them I didn't do this!"

Jake tries to speak, but seeing Mark there, and remembering what he just saw in the Dutchman's room minutes before…and he can't. He opens his mouth, closes it, makes to try again, and then shakes his head that he cannot. Then Mark's eyes go wide as he sees his father's best friend standing there all of a sudden.

"What is going on, Mark," Carl says, stepping forward before Jake has a chance to speak, "is that you've killed your father. He's been found dead in his quarters, a gunshot to the head, and your pistol sitting right on the bedside table next to him."

"Right on the…" Mark repeats, then looks back to Carl. "Can't you see this is all a hoax, all made up? My God – I've been framed!"

"When we run ballistics I've no doubt that we'll find the bullet matches the gun, and your hand will show the powder residue indicating you fired it."

Mark rolls his eyes. "Of *course* my hand will have the powder residue on it – I was just firing the damn thing in Dulce not 12 hours ago!"

"Tell it to the JAG," Carl says, then looks to the base guards. "Get him up and get him out of here."

"No, this is a set-up!" Mark shouts as the guards get him to his feet, get his hands cuffed, and start taking him from the room.

Jake stands there, watching it all happen. He'd heard the guards rushing down the hallway from his room, had stuck his head out to check. They'd only been a few doors down from him so he'd popped his head in, and that's when he'd seen the Dutchman. Carl came soon after, saw the gun, and put two and two together. Now Mark was being hauled-off down the hallway, protesting to anyone who'd listen.

"Shame what he did," Carl says as he starts to the door, pauses to talk to Jake. "All that time off-world musta warped his brain."

"Right," Jake says distantly, his thoughts elsewhere.

"You get some rest, Jake…you like mighty tired."

"Will do, sir," Jake says in that same tone, and this time Carl gives him a clap on the shoulder and walks back into the hallway.

Jake is left standing there, wondering…worrying. *Something's not right,* he thinks*, something is* very *not right.*

"Donlon will know what to do," he says to himself. He goes back out into the hallway, intent on finding the man.

PART III

10 – NEW REALITIES

Area 51
Friday, May 25, 1982
12:25 AM

Turn comes out of the gate and into a room with concrete walls, a concrete floor, and a large meeting table in its center. It looks like a conference room, he thinks, but then turns his head and sees several rows of desks. It looks like a classroom too, complete with a blackboard on one wall, even some of those pull-down maps he remembers from high school. Ahead of him is Bennewitz. Then from behind him comes Walter.

"Sorry about that," the captain says, referring to the push he gave Turn to get him through the gate, "but like I said, you had to see for yourself."

Turn shrugs it off, then asks, "Where are we?"

"A safe place," Bennewitz replies.

"Yeah, but *where?*"

"Might be better to ask, 'when'," Walter says.

Turn's eyes narrow at that, but before he can say anything else, Bennewitz speaks up.

"We're at Area 51, which in the current time we're in, *is* a safe place." He looks Turn in the eye. "That time is the year 1982."

"*1982?*" Turn says. "What the hell?"

"We have to hop around," Bennewitz says, hitting a few buttons on the control panel near the shimmering gateway they'd just come through, then looking back to him, "no one place is safe for long."

"We're being hunted through both space *and* time," Walter says with a chuckle, though when Turn meets his eyes he sees no humor there.

"So we hop around" Bennewitz says again. "Before I came to Dulce tonight, I did so from 1988 via 1981 and then to your 1979 before coming back through 1982 here."

"And then where?" Turn asks, thinking right away that he probably should have said 'then when.'

"A lot of that depends on what happens at Blue Lake following the attack on Dulce," Walter says, glancing down at his watch. "By now Ellis should be giving his debriefing, and soon after that the pieces of the chessboard will begin to move about." When Turn looks confused, he says, "The traitors, Turn…the high-ranking military officers that are working with the Grays and in turn the Reptilians."

"Lot to digest, I know," Bennewitz says as he begins to hit a few more buttons. Walter too sees that Turn has taken a lot in, and he moves over to watch Bennewitz. Turn just goes into his thoughts.

Traitors?

Turn's eyes narrow as he thinks back to that day in the barracks right after their Montana mission.

"Yeah, but don't you think it's funny that none of the briefings we had over the past week or so have mentioned why the Grays are here, why they broke that treaty, and why we need to get back into that base so bad?" Lewie had said at the time. Turn remembers it because Tommy had answered by saying, *"You know why,"* and in the calmest voice Turn had ever heard the joker use.

Lewie had been about to say something but then Carl had suddenly strolled into the room, cutting the chatter off. *Carl*, Turn thinks, *the man closest to the Dutchman…and perhaps one that means him harm. But I need proof, damn it!* he thinks to himself, but he knows that'll be hard to find.

Dulce Base is just the tip of the iceberg," Bennewitz says, drawing Turn back from his thoughts.

Turn's eyes narrow. "What do you mean?"

"He means," Walter says, strolling over to the side of the room and drawing both men's attention as he does so, "that Dulce is just one hub in a vast network of underground tunnels which honeycomb our planet." He looks to Bennewitz. "How 'bout we pull down the map?" and nods at something above his head before reaching up to the kind of maps that Turn remembers from grade school, all rolled up in a bunch at the top of the center blackboard, just waiting to be unfurled one at a time to illuminate the young children's understanding of the world. Walter grabs hold of one of the metal handles at the end of one map and pulls. A map comes down, one that Turn had certainly never seen in his public education days. He stands there staring at it, not sure what he's looking at.

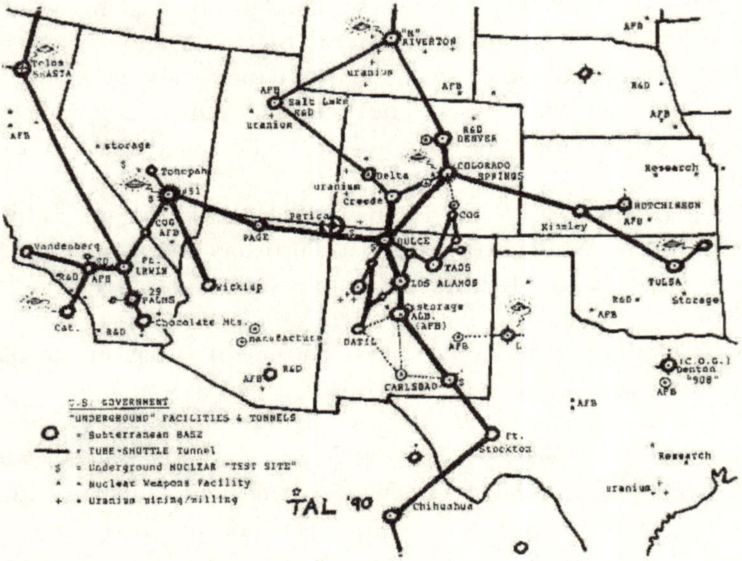

"As you can see," Bennewitz continues behind Walter, strolling forward to get up close to the map, though he stays away from it and crosses his arms, staring up at it, "there are tunnels stretching all over the southwest, and we've got other maps showing the rest of the country, and the world."

"And each of those tunnels has tracks which carry the same tube trains that brought us into Dulce," Walter says.

"*God*," Turn says, staring at the map, "there must be a dozen bases just in the Four Corners region!"

"Not bases," Bennewitz says, stepping forward to tap at the map, "but stations. Underground connecting stations, to be exact. The aliens use 'em when they come down from space, docking their ships and getting onto the trains. That way they can conduct their business here on Earth without ever having to step on the surface of the planet, and without ever having to fly their ships around where we can all see 'em."

"What about other places, Paul?" Walter asks. "Are there other sites tied-in to this 'shuttle network' other than those which you've just mentioned?"

"Yeah, and if so, where *are* these entrances?" Turn chimes-in.

Bennewitz chuckles. "Where? *Where?* Why…they're *every*where, that's where! They crisscross the world as an endless subterranean highway system, kinda like a freeway except this one's totally underground. It's got miles and miles of paved roads for cars and trucks and even busses, and then there's the track system for the trains."

He scoffs. "There's *thousands* of miles of that, *tens* of thousands. The trains carry both passengers and freight and collectively this underground network is called the 'Sub-Global System.'"

"Catchy," Turn says dryly and with a roll of the eyes.

"And *catching*," Bennewitz continues, giving a nod Turn's way. "Those that use the underground system *never* want to go back to the old, aboveground ones. And can you blame 'em? After you've taken a flight across the Atlantic, why would you ever want to take a slow-moving ship across again?"

"You wouldn't," Walter agrees.

"How do they power those trains?" Turn asks, getting his question in quick before Bennewitz can get started again.

Bennewitz nods. "Maglev technology and the vacuum method. Both allow the tube trains to travel faster than the speed of sound."

"A global system like that must have entrances all over the place then," Turn points out.

"It does," Bennewitz says. "Here in America you'll find 'em in every state of the union. Most times the entrances are camouflaged as sand quarries or mining operations. Other, more complex entrance portals are found on military bases. And most of those bases are right here, in the South- and Midwest. New Mexico and Arizona have the largest number of entrances, followed by California, Montana, Idaho, Colorado, Pennsylvania, Kansas, Arkansas and Missouri. Of all the states, Florida and North Dakota have the least. Wyoming, being as rural and low-populated as she is, has a road that opens *directly* into the subterranean freeway."

"You're kiddin'!" Turn says with a laugh.

"Wish I was," Bennewitz replies. "The good news is that the road is no longer in use, although it *could* be reactivated if they decide to do so…and with minimal cost. It's located near Brooks Lake, and who knows, the way things are going, maybe we'll need it."

"Maybe," Walter agrees, "but for now we've got to focus on the treachery taking place at Blue Lake." He looks to Turn. "Something's about to go down, we know of it, and now we just have to wait for it to happen."

"And then what?" Turn says, figuring he'd save himself a lot of time and grief if he just played along and didn't ask for explanations.

Bennewitz laughs. "Why, then we ride in to save the day!"

11 – IMPRISONED

Blue Lake
Friday, May 25, 1979
8:34 AM

Mark stares venom at the door, and he hopes whoever comes through it next would see that look. So far no one *had* come, however, no one since the guards had brought him into this small room. There was little there – Mark's chair, a rickety metal desk against one wall, a single chair for it, and then a few file cabinets and cardboard boxes. They'd taken the cuffs from one hand, put another set onto that hand, then they'd locked both of them to the metal chair that Mark was now sitting in. That'd been an hour ago…maybe longer. All Mark could do during that time was fret and fume, and wonder at who had set him up.

Aaron…Carl…perhaps someone I don't even know?

Aaron was a good candidate for their traitor, that much was clear. Mark's mind shot back to that moment in the Dulce port when Aaron had told him of Johnny's death, Andy's freak-out, and Turn rushing back into the base. Mark had wanted to go back, for he'd never left two men behind before and he hadn't been about to start. But then Aaron had grabbed him by the arm, looked into his eyes, and told him in no uncertain terms that yes, the men were in fact dead. A*nd you will be too if we don't get out of here, we* all *will be*, Aaron had said.

Now Mark knew it was all a lie, that Aaron was in fact a traitor to their cause and probably not the only one. Well, he liked to *think* that was the case. The truth of the matter was that he just didn't know.

With a sigh Mark shakes the thoughts away. Speculation would do him little good at the moment, the same as yelling or banging on the door. He'd tried both soon after being put in the room – yelling was easiest, moving the chair over to the door to bang on it took a little more work – but both efforts proved equally futile. So Mark sat, and waited, and worried. Not a minute after doing so and their were footfalls outside the door, then the knob was turning. The door opens, and Carl appears.

"Mark," he says matter-of-factly as he comes in, alone and with no base guards with him.

"Carl," Mark replies, using that same cold and emotionless tone. Carl comes in and heads for the desk, taking the chair and then leaning back to put his hands behind his head. He sits there a moment, staring at Mark. Then he speaks.

"Why'd you do it, Mark? Why'd you kill Ellis?"

Mark rolls his eyes. "You and I both know that never happened."

"Do you really think it's going to be that easy?" Carl asks with a laugh.

"Easier," Mark says with a sneer.

Carl chuckles, then starts shaking his head. "You *are* stubborn, aren't you? Just as stubborn as your father was."

"The truth of his death will come out."

"*What*…that a jealous son finally got his old hatreds out by offing the old man?" Carl scoffs. "Your prints are on the gun and my men are heading-up the investigation. It's an open and shut case."

"You killed him," Mark says, looking straight in Carl's eyes. "You killed him and you covered it up...but like all cover-ups, there's *someone* who knows, *something* you didn't think of."

Carl cocks his head to one side, as if acceding the point. "You're right on the first part, or at least you *were* right." Mark's eyes narrow in confusion, and Carl can see the first hint that the man's confidence is beginning to falter. "Don't believe me?" he continues, and walks over to the desk and retrieves a small rectangular control of some sort. He points it at the wall, clicks a button on it, and a panel on the wall begins to slide away to reveal a large TV-like monitor. "Don't take *my* word for it," Carl says as he pushes another button and a video begins to play, one showing General Anderholt and Aaron, "take a look with your own eyes."

12 – ALLIES

Blue Lake
Friday, May 25, 1979
8:50 AM

Jake bursts into the rec room and comes to a stop, his hands on his hips. He's breathing hard, for he's just run down several of the Blue Lake hallways to get here. The rec room was in a different area of the base than the officer's quarters were, and the latter had been the place that Jake had seen Mark at when he'd been taken away. He knew he had to do something about that, even if 'doing' only meant telling someone.

"*Whoa* there," a voice calls out to him as he stands there, "where's the fire, eh?"

Jake turns his head and sees Bobbie sitting over at a card table on the side of the room, a few of the regular base guards with him. By the looks of it they're in the middle of a game of poker or something, chips piled up in front of them…though most seem to be centered in front of Bobbie.

Without a word, Jake nods and starts that way. Besides the four at the card table, the room is empty…of people, that is. There's an old pool table in the center of the room, a pinball machine on one side. A ping pong table takes up another good portion, and then it's just some old couches and chairs in front of a TV that looks to be from the 50s. Jake doesn't register any of it as he heads to the table.

"Listen, I gotta find Donlon," he says as he reaches it. His words are for everyone, but mostly directed at Bobbie.

Bobbie's face screws up. "Why Donlon?" He scoffs. "Hell, that guy's about as dry an' borin' as they come!" That elicits a few chuckles and nods from some of the base guards.

"Knows his stuff too, and doesn't let his mouth get in the way of him doin' a good job." Jake casts a narrow-eyed look Bobbie's way as he says that, raises an eyebrow to accentuate his words. Bobbie just smirks and dismisses the comment with a wave of his hand.

"Alright, *fine*, have it you're way…last I saw Donlon was in the debriefing, same as you."

"Didn't see where he went? He's not in the officer's quarters."

Bobbie laughs and throws up his arms in the classic 'I dunno' gesture.

"Well, *hell!*" Jake says, and with a sigh and a roll of the eyes, he turns around in frustration, slapping one hand against his thigh.

"Jake, what's up?" Bobbie says now, a bit more concern in his voice. When Jake turns back around he sees that the young super soldier has even put his cards down to look up at him concernedly.

"Can I have a minute?" Jake says, and after narrowing his eyes for a moment, Bobbie nods and starts to get up from the table. The two men move across the room to stand near the pinball machine, a large window looking out onto one of the base's tarmacs giving them ample light.

"What's–" Bobbie starts, but Jake cuts him off.

"Mark's been taken and the Dutchman is dead," he says.

"What the–" Bobbie starts to say, and loudly, but then he glances around and lowers his voice "What the *fuck?*"

"Carl was there in Mark's room when I just happened to walk by," Jake continues. "Carl says that Mark killed his father."

"You believe that?" Bobbie asks, his face screwing up in disgust.

"Not for one second," says Jake.

"Then that means we've got a setup here, and though I hate to say it when aliens are involved, a conspiracy as well."

"And that's why I gotta find Donlon."

"Why not Chargin' Charlie…or even General Anderholt?"

"Because I don't know who to trust, that's why!"

"But you know you can trust Donlon?" Bobbie chuckles. "Hell, Charlie was there in the thick of it with us too, ya know."

"Yeah, I know, it's just…"

"Just what?"

"I dunno, Bobbie, it's just…I dunno!"

Bobbie rolls his eyes to that, but seeing how much pressure and anxiety Jake seems to be under, he holds his tongue, and instead puts his hand forth and claps his friend on the shoulder.

"Take it easy, Jake – Donlon's around and you'll find him. Until then…mind if I get back to my game of cards?" Jake looks over and sees some of the base guards giving the two of them funny looks, and he nods. "Great," Bobbie continues, turning away and starting to walk back to the table, though he says over his shoulder, "I'll keep my eyes out for Donlon, get word to you as soon as I do."

Jake nods to that, and then a moment later heads back out into the hallways, back out into the troubled world of the Blue Lake base.

13 – PAST THE STARS

Blue Lake
Friday, May 25, 1979
9:12 AM

Carl sits at the desk in the small room, frowning at Mark. So far the man has said nothing…likely because of what he just saw on the video monitor, the conversation between Aaron and General Anderholt. Looking at Mark, Carl knows he can't believe it, but he can't discount what his own eyes and ears have just told him, either. Clearly, there are traitors at the top. Carl knows that's what's going through Mark's mind, and that's what's keeping him in quiet contemplation. Still, Carl has ways of making him talk.

"Now, before we get much further," Carl says, leaning forward once again to look at Mark, "there are some things I want you to tell me."

"I'm not telling you shit."

"Things about off-world affairs," Carl says, ignoring the comment, "things about what's *really* going on out there between the Grays and Reptilians, the Sirians and especially the Collective."

"What part of, 'I'm not telling you shit' didn't you understand?" Mark says.

This time Carl turns and looks him in the eye. "All of it." He turns back around, heads to a metal desk at the wall. "Now, do *you* want to talk, or do you want *this* to do the talking for you." Carl turns back around, and this time he's holding a large syringe. Mark doesn't need to be told what it is, but Carl tells him anyway. "Sodium pentothal…truth serum."

Mark says nothing, just sits there stone-faced.

"Not so glib anymore, are you?" Carl says, scoffing. "And you know what, I think we won't take any chances today."

"You're–" Mark starts to say, but Carl jabs the needle down into his thigh, pushes the plunger with his thumb. Both men watch as the liquid goes into Mark, all of it.

"Now," Carl says, taking as step back and brushing back his closely-cropped and graying hair, "let's start with an easy one, a *close* one." He sits down in the roller-chair opposite Mark. "Tell me about Black Knight. What does it know…what is it sending out?"

"*Black Knight?"* Mark says, his face screwing up in confusion. "No one controls that…no one on Earth, at least."

"But someone is…who?"

Mark shrugs, and Carl frowns. He wishes the truth serum was taking effect, but it takes time. He decides to take a different approach.

"I've got a team working to take it over."

"*Take it…*" Mark starts, before chuckling. "What the hell are you gonna do with that ol' clunker?"

"We'll use its instantaneous download feature to send a reverse signal, though one with a net attached. On the other end of the line, the Sirians will never know what hit 'em." Carl frowns and shakes his head. "I just wish it wasn't so damn far away."

"Around Arcturus, that's where the signal's coming from, right?"

"Yes. Arcturus is another star in the Boötes system. In ancient Mesopotamia the star was associated with the god Enlil." Carl chuckles. "The New Agers think that Arcturus is the gateway for the soul to take once it leaves the body, and perhaps they were right once…but not anymore."

"No," Mark scoffs, "now you steal those souls before they can even make it past the planet's outer magnetically-charged energy field."

"You must admit that it's efficient," Carl says, looking down at his nails for a moment before looking back at Mark. "In the five years that we've had the system fully up and operational, we've had an 84% success rate when it comes to soul capture."

"*Soul capture*, is that what you call it?"

"You have a better name?'

"How 'bout 'hell'?"

Carl laughs. "Oh, Mark…always the fighter, even when it's clear you've lost. In that way you're no different from your father."

"So in those five years, how many souls do you think you've stolen?" Mark asks changing the subject, trying to get as much information as he can. Carl senses this, and begins to grow bored with the conversation.

"Millions," he says, "now, why don't we–"

"You'll never make it work," Mark says quickly.

"No?" Carl mocks him. "You seem to forget that the Grays have spent the past twenty or more years cementing their presence here – and they're just working for the Reptilians! All the abductions, all the impregnations…it all leads to one thing – a hybrid race that humans can't tell apart from their own. Eventually those hybrids will have the reins of government firmly in their control." He cocks his head to one side in a shrug. "They already do, really, what with the Rockefeller's and their foundation, as well as the all the influence coming from Kissinger." He sighs. "But I grow bored of this conversation, one that's giving me nothing." He looks down at his watch. "I'll be back in twenty minutes when the serum has taken full effect."

Without another word Carl turns on his heel and heads out of the room, leaving Mark stuck to that chair, a vile toxin coursing through his veins.

14 – BLACK KNIGHT

Area 51
Friday, May 25, 1982
1:07 AM

The three men sit at the large conference table, no one saying anything. Most sit staring at the table or the floor or twiddling their thumbs…waiting for the right time. Finally Bennewitz shakes his head and looks over at Walter. "Could be the Black Knight Satellite again."

"Oh, God…let's hope not," Walter replies with a groan.

"*Black Knight?*" Turn says, one eyebrow cocked. "Uh…guys, remember – I don't have the foggiest idea of what you're talking about."

Bennewitz looks to Walter. "You want to explain it, or should I?"

"Be my guest," Walter replies, whereupon Bennewitz nods and looks back to Turn.

"Came about back in March, 1960," he says. "*TIME* Magazine ran a story on the Dark Fence radar program and how three weeks earlier they'd found an object orbiting above the continental US. Well, it was determined that it was a dark satellite, for the main reason that it wasn't transmitting any signals that we could detect."

"It was just *floating* there?" Turn says, and Bennewitz nods.

"Just floating. At first we figured it had to be the Russians, for who else is gonna be launching satellites up into orbit…*and* keep them right over our roofs lookin' down?" He scoffs. "We knew it wasn't Russian for the simple reason that it was in a polar orbit."

"Polar orbit?" Walter repeats. "But…but…we couldn't pass over both the north *and* south poles once per revolution until…"

"1965," Bennewitz says, nodding. "Neither we nor the Russians could do that twenty years ago, but here was a satellite that *was* doing it."

A silence falls as both men let Turn digest the words. Bennewitz picks it up after a brief pause of ten seconds.

"Six months later in September 1960 the Grumman Aircraft Corporation managed to get some images of the thing. Their Long Island factory snapped a photo of a reddish-pink glowing object that was moving in an east-to-west orbit…something that was the complete opposite of what most man-made satellites did, which was to orbit north-to-south."

"Also means it couldn't have been doing the polar orbit that Time Magazine said it was," Walter says.

Bennewitz nods. "Wouldn't be until three years later – in May, 1963 – that astronaut Gordon Cooper caught a first-hand glimpse of the satellite when he was doing his 22-orbit Mercury-Atlas 9 flight. Said it was glowing neon green and that it was larger than any man-made satellite that he'd ever seen."

"That's not all, either," Bennewitz says after a brief pause, one in which Turn's eyes are narrowed, his brow furrowed, and all sense of what is possible and impossible in the world has gone from him.

"Oh?" the super soldier says, shocked that there could be more.

"Back at the time it was first discovered by Time a bunch o' ham radio operators started to say they were getting weird radio signals. One in particular even said that he'd received a signal that, once he'd decoded it, said the message's origin was a place called Epsilon Boötis."

When Turn's eyes narrowed even further in confusion, Walter speaks.

"Epsilon Boötis is 203 light years from Earth. The message that the ham radio operator decoded supposedly came to us 13,000 years ago."

"There's more" Bennewitz says. "That ham operator was a Scottish science fiction author and he also dabbled in astronomy. He wrote up his findings, sent them off to the British Interplanetary Society, and they published them up in their magazine. What was so interesting is that he claimed the exact same signal that he'd found – the one telling us of Epsilon Boötis – was actually discovered forty years earlier, in the 1920s."

"Group of researchers were looking into the long delayed echo effect back then, Walter says, picking up the story again, "but they dismissed it as an echo of an Earth-originating signal that was simply bouncing off the moon. Forty years later our Scottish sci-fi author does not, however, and he decodes a message telling us that…" he trails-off and looks around for a few moments, finally focusing back on Bennewitz. "Isn't there a–"

"On the computer," Bennewitz says, reading Walter's mind. He goes to the nearest console, does a few quick keystrokes, and sits back after a few moments to stare at his handiwork. "Here it is."

Both Turn and Walter head over to the computer and read what's there. Bennewitz reads it aloud.

"Start here. Our home is Upsilon Boötis, which is a double star. We live on the sixth planet of seven, coming from the sun, which is the larger of the two. Our sixth planet has one moon. Our fourth planet has three. Our first and third planets each have one. Our probe is in the position of Arcturus, known in our maps."

"Wow!" Turn says.

"And that's not even the half of it," Walter says before glancing at Bennewitz. "Should I tell him about Philip K. Dick?"

"The *author?"* Turn says, his face screwing up in confusion even more, if that's at all possible. Turn can't remember the last time he was as flummoxed as he is now.

"The author," Bennewitz confirms. "Back in '74 he got zapped by an information-rich beam of pink light, one that came directly from the Black Knight Satellite. This created all kinds of awakenings in Dick, so much so that he was able to glean a deeper understanding of the Vast Active Living Intelligence System of the universe, or what he termed VALIS." He cocked his head to one side in a kind of shrug. "In two years he'll have a book out about it."

"VALIS and our idea of 'God' can be thought of interchangeably," Walter says.

"And it all comes back to the soul catchers," Bennewitz says.

"Sure does," Walter agrees, "though hopefully Tommy's death won't be in vain."

"Damn well better not be," Bennewitz says, nodding, "and I'm sure Stu will see to that."

"Whoa, guys…" Turn says, giving the men a wry look, "could ya maybe fill me in on what the hell you're talking about here, please?"

Bennewitz chuckles and walks over and claps Turn on the shoulder. "I sometimes forget that you're not fully 'in-the-know'," he says. "For now, just realize that when we die, our souls aren't going to Heaven but are instead being stolen to feed the Gray's insatiable appetite for that soulful energy."

"Soulful energy?" Turn says.

Bennewitz laughs. "Don't worry – it ain't some James Brown song we're talkin' about here, just the fate of the universe."

"And one man knows that fate better than anyone," Walter says, looking over at Bennewitz.

Bennewitz nods. "Time to bust him out."

15 – TRAITORS

Blue Lake
Friday, May 25, 1979
9:34 AM

Jake has searched high and low, but he can't find Donlon anywhere on the base. He's run into a few of the others he'd fought beside down in Dulce, but they were about as much help as Bobbie had been, which was to say not much. Jake won't give up, though, and continues down the base hallways, poking his head in meeting rooms and labs and every office that presented itself. In one of those offices he comes face to face with General Anderholt.

"Uh…sorry, sir," Jake says as soon as he opens the door, takes a step in, and then sees the general. He immediately starts to turn around.

"Hold up there, Jake," Anderholt says. Jake is surprised that the general still knows his name. It was quite a few years ago that he woke up in that hospital room with the general sitting there at the end of his bed. Since that time Jake had seen things he never could have imagined. He didn't regret it for one second.

"Yes, sir?" Jake says, turned about now. Before him, Anderholt leans back in his chair and takes the still-smoldering cigar from the ashtray on the desk, begins to smoke it back to life.

"Have you heard about what happened to Mark and Ellis?"

"Yes…yes, sir. I was there when Carl took Mark away."

"Oh?" Anderholt says, as if this surprises him, which it does not.

Jake nods. "Was passing by at the time, heard the commotion and saw the soldiers and figured I'd check to see if everything was alright. Then I pop my head into the room and lying on the floor is the Dutchman, er…Ellis…and he's dead."

"And then what?"

Jake shrugs. "I was in shock, and when Carl – he was the one that was in charge – picked up the gun that was near Ellis's head he said right away, 'this is Mark's gun.' Well, after that he turned the base guards loose and we headed to Mark's room. We found him there, in bed with one of the women we saved from Dulce, and after taking her away Mark was taken away as well." Jake shakes his head at this point and lets out a sigh. "Sir, I'm not sure *what's* going on, but it sure doesn't seem right to me. I mean…Mark killing his own father? I just don't buy it, sir."

"You're smart not to," Anderholt replies, and then leans back in his chair and looks up at the ceiling. After a few moments of that he leans forward, stubs out his cigar, and then folds his hands together atop his desk. He stares at Jake intently. Finally he shrugs, cocking his eyebrows as he does so, and slowly begins to shake his head before meeting Jake's eyes. "Jake, you've seen too much."

Jake's eyes narrow, but he doesn't say a word. He's starting to get a bad feeling about this, however, and wonders if telling the general his thoughts was such a good idea after all. *Surely Anderholt can't be in on it…can he?* Jake thinks to himself as the general gets his cigar put out and leaves it in the ashtray.

"You've seen too much and there's just no way we can trust you not to keep looking for answers…like you are now."

Jake narrows his eyes. "What do you mean, sir?"

"I mean, your use here has run its course, son." Anderholt reaches below him to a desk drawer he'd already pulled out. Reaching inside, his fingers fall on what he's seeking and he wraps his hand around it.

"My…*use*?" Jake says, confused.

"Oh, Jake…*why'd* you have to ask so many questions?" Anderholt pulls his arm up, and there in his hand is a flashgun. Jake's eyes go wide.

"Sir," he says, taking a step back and putting one hand up in front of him, "sir…don't do this."

"Do what…" Anderholt asks, "…push this button here and vaporize you into a little pile of ash?"

He has his head cocked to one side as he points down at that button on the flashgun, his eyes going back up to Jake as he finishes. For his part, Jake just stands there, like a deer caught in headlights and unable to move. Then just like that, he decides he'll make a break for it. He dashes to his left, with the plan to swivel, get down, then get that door open. If he can just–

ZAP!

Anderholt presses the button he'd been pointing at and a laser-like 'flash' shoots out, hitting Jake right in the back. And just like that, the soldier winks out of existence, nothing to show for his life but that little pile of ash Anderholt had mentioned earlier.

"Oh, Jake, Jake, Jake," the general says as he gets up, walking around his desk to look at the pile of ash that was once one of the most decorated heroes from the war in Afghanistan. That war was still another 22 years away, not here in good ol' 1979 but in the year 2001. That's where Jake had been from, and once again Anderholt knew his decision of twenty years ago to use soldiers not from this time was one of the best ideas he'd ever had.

No one will miss them, he'd thought at the time, and he thinks that now as he bends over the small pile of ash and blows. The remains of Jake blow toward the doorway and collect at the edges of the filing cabinet, with some even clinging stubbornly to the floor. Anderholt leaves them there, smiling at the thought of the janitor mopping them away later.

No one will miss him, Anderholt thinks again as he returns to his desk and retrieves a fresh cigar, *no one at all.*

16 – BEHIND THE CURTAIN

Blue Lake
Friday, May 25, 1979
9:47 AM

The doorknob begins to turn and Mark looks at it wearily. With blurry vision he sees it open, then two figures come in. He can't make them out, but figures one must be Carl.

"It's been twenty minutes," Mark says, a bit sluggishly like he's coming out of anesthesia.

"Twenty-four, actually," Carl says, glancing down at his watch, then, "Has the truth serum taken effect yet, Mark?"

"Six minutes ago," Mark replies, drowsily trying to focus on the two men. He finally does so, and what he sees sends something else coursing through his veins – anger. The adrenaline-fueled emotion isn't enough to overwhelm the sodium pentothal, but it does awaken him and give him back a bit of his senses. There before him, and standing next to Carl, is General Anderholt.

"Hell, Mark," the general says, "it's good to see you again…though under the circumstances…"

He trails-off, shaking his head after a moment. Then he looks to Carl. "I thought I told you not to kill his father."

Carl shrugs. "Had to be done, and besides…now we have Mark here to pin the murder on."

"Pin the…how the hell are you gonna do that when he's dead?"

Carl can only give another shrug, to which Anderholt can only scoff and shake his head. A moment later he turns back to Mark. "Well, no use cryin' over spilled milk. Now, shall we get this round of questioning underway, Carl, or what?"

"Yes, sir," Carl replies, a wicked smile on his face.

"You killed my father," Mark says before Carl can begin however, then, looking at Anderholt, "and you're in on it, you bastard."

"Now, now, Mark, you just need to *calm* down, that's all."

Mark casts a hateful look Anderholt's way. "The truth will come out, it always does."

Anderholt smiles. "What…your father's murder, or the real reason you came back…because of events unfolding, events most everyone on Earth has no idea about?" He laughs. "You know the corporate structure, Mark, and you know it'd *never* allow such a thing to happen."

"You make it sound like you're *so* special," Mark says with a chuckle, "but you're not. You really have no power left, not after the changes that've occurred. No," he laughs now, "you and the rest of MJ12 are now at the *bottom* of the pecking order."

"Oh?" Anderholt says, a slightly bemused smile edging one corner of his mouth.

"The Ultra unit…the Blue Moon unit…hell, even Alpha One and Alpha Two are above you now!" Mark laughs, enjoying that slight smile slip from Anderholt's face. "You're not the top dogs anymore, and I think you know it. Do you and your cronies discuss that while meeting at your precious country club, you know, the one in the mountains outside Warrington, Virginia?"

The slight smile on Anderholt's face is replaced by a sneer. It stays there for several moments, but then disappears and is replaced by a slight smile.

"You won't get *me* riled, Mark…I'm not your father." Mark only sneers at Anderholt in return, while Carl just leans against the wall, watching the two go at it. "But what we really want to know, Mark, and what we gave you that serum for," Anderholt continues, pacing the small room a bit, "is what kind of resistance is mounting to the Reptilian plan here? Is the Collective mounting something…or have they, and you're it?"

He says that last with a smile, and Mark wants to tell him that yes, he is it, but the serum won't allow it.

"They know of what's going on, and as you believe, they don't approve. As for mounting a resistance, well…it hasn't happened yet."

"Too busy arguing with one another in their halls of power, eh?" Anderholt says, and Mark nods despite himself.

"Why'd you do it, if you're on they're side? Why'd you destroy Dulce Base?"

"Simple," Anderholt says, "the Reptilians wanted it that way." When Mark narrows his eyes, Anderholt smiles and paces the room a bit. "You see, Mark, the Grays at Dulce got away from the Reptilians, started to make the place their own. Remember, the Reptilians are the *true* power on this planet, have been for millennia. Well, after that events of '75, the Grays thought they might be able to get out from under the Reptilians' thumb. They did a good job of it too…for about five years." Anderholt shrugs. "Then the Reptilians decided to let the Grays remember who was *really* in charge."

"And now they know?" Mark asks.

Anderholt nods. "Sure do. That attack sent 'em scurryin', both to what underground bases they deem safe here on Earth, *and* to their bases on the dark side of the moon."

"What about the motherships?"

"What about you let me worry about them?" Anderholt says.

"Lotta questions," Carl says.

"There always is…before they give in," Anderholt replies.

Mark scoffs. "What…go over to your side? Never!"

"You just can't beat 'em, Mark," Carl says. "I spent years trying to convince your father of that, but no, he'd have none of it." Carl shakes his head. "Year after year, mission after mission, one team of young boys after another…and for what? My God, Mark – can't you see that they've won already, did so back in '54 when Ike signed that deal with 'em?"

"Carl's right," Anderholt says as Mark sits there, looking bewildered. "I saw the truth of it years ago, even before that treaty was signed at Holloman. I saw it the day I stumbled upon Dulce, a pimple-faced colonel fresh off a' World War Two." The general chuckles. "It was clear to me then, and it should damn well be clear to you, Mark, what with all the time you've spent off-world. *You* know how many worlds the Reptilians have destroyed, *you* know how many in the Collective say that they're unstoppable, that they should just be left to their own devices."

"And they're wrong," Mark says. "You and the others working

with them will find that out firsthand, and you won't like it."

"*Working* with them? Carl says with a chuckle. "Mark, you have *no* idea."

He nods after saying the words, and Mark glances over his shoulder to see one of the base guards nod as well. After that the man turns around and hits something on the wall, perhaps a hidden button there. The wall begins to slide away, revealing an open doorway. From that doorway comes a Gray, its long spindly arms reaching down well past its waist, those big black eyes as empty and lifeless as ever. Mark is in shock, but not as much as he finds himself in a moment later. After the Gray steps into the room, a Reptilian comes into view behind it. The creature's snout is long and scaled, and as it opens Mark can see two long rows of razor sharp teeth. The Reptilian gnashes those teeth, emitting a guttural series of sounds in the process. Besides that it has a flashgun in one hand…as if it needs the thing. Mark also glances at those razor sharp claws on its hands, claws that can rip a man's face off in one clean swipe.

The Gray shifts a little on its feet a moment after that, seemingly directing its attention to Carl. Then Carl nods, and as he turns from the Gray back to Mark, a smile edges up one corner of his mouth.

"It tells me you're filing all this information away, planning on how to use it later to stop us." Carl chuckles. "As if there's gonna *be* a 'later'."

"There will be," Mark says, giving a hard look Carl's way before doing the same to Anderholt and even the two aliens present, "there's no way you're going to cover up my father's murder, *or* pin his death on me. Too many people will ask questions. Dad had too many friends."

"You mean friends like Carl?" Anderholt says, chuckling for a moment as he rolls his eyes. "No, Mark, I'm not worried about anyone talking, for who would they talk to? Carl here…maybe a base guard?" He chuckles again. "No, I think it's *far* more likely they'll come straight to me, the top rank on this base…don't you?"

When Anderholt looks at him, Mark just rolls his eyes and looks down to the floor. Hearing the general speak is making him sick. Anderholt laughs and continues speaking.

"'Cover up your father's death,' you say? Why, Mark…why would I need to do that when I can pin it on you? And hould anyone come and ask, I can pin it on them. Hell, the more I look at it like that, it might be best just to kill you now!" He chuckles. "There are lots of dumb flyboys like you that'll unwittingly take the blame, when the evidence I plant leads to them, that is."

"You'll never kill me," Mark says. "You need me for whatever plan you have. With me dead people will begin asking who killed my father, and who killed me."

"I'm not worried about that, Mark, because I have your friend Jake to pin the blame on."

"*Jake?"* Mark says. "What's he got to do with this?"

"Saw you taken away, went around talking, and then made the mistake of coming to see me." Anderholt chuckles as he looks down at the gun in his hand. "He said we had traitors in our midst, ones that might go all the way to the top."

He looks over at Carl as he says that last, and both men have a good laugh. A moment later Anderholt turns back to Mark. "So when he told me everything, I simply couldn't believe this opportunity – a real life patsy just knockin' on my door." The smile fades and is replaced with seriousness. "Pulled a gun out right then and there and zapped him. Poof – he's no more!"

Mark turns away, sickened at what he's hearing. Anderholt and Carl just laugh, while the two aliens stand by looking impatient and the base guards ignore it all.

"Killin' him might make more sense…if you really can pin it all on Jake," Carl says.

"And why can't I pin it all on him? Hell, I recruited him into this program, I brought him into this timeframe – why *can't* I do with him as I please?"

Anderholt looks over at Carl, but the man only shrugs, as if to say, 'sounds fine by me, boss.'

"You know, the more I think of it…" Anderholt says as he reaches into his jacket pocket and pulls out a flashgun, "…why not? Why not take out both of the Richards in one day?"

He points the flashgun at Mark, a sinister smile coming to his face.

PART IV

17 – OUT OF TIME

Blue Lake
Friday, May 25, 1979
10:07 AM

Mark stares at the flashgun pointing at him, knowing he's about to die.

"Any last words?" Anderholt asks, a smirk on his face.

"Yeah, I'll see you in Hell."

Anderholt scoffs and then looks over at the Reptilian before looking back to Mark. "You know, maybe being zapped into nothingness is too kind. Perhaps having your face ripped off would be better."

He looks back to the Reptilian and nods. The Reptilian gives about as close to it can come to a smile, and takes another step forward. Mark closes his eyes and silently begins to pray.

BZZ…ZZB…BZZ…

Mark opens his eyes at the sound. It's the unmistakable sound of a teleporter keying-in to their very spot! He looks up and sees both Anderholt's and Carl's brows furrowing, a confused look coming to their faces. Even the Reptilian looks confused, as well as the Grays standing by the door.

BZZ…ZZB…BZZ…*POOF!*

The sound comes again, this time with some lighting crackles accompanying it, and then the teleportation gateway opens. It's a shimmering silver and black cloud seemingly suspended in midair over nothing, while in reality it's a gateway to another place, perhaps even another time. Mark had teleported many times in his long and varied career, so knew what was coming next…just not who.

The 'who' turned out to be Walter, followed quickly by…Paul Bennewitz – he can't believe his eyes! Right after that comes one of the super soldiers that'd gone into Dulce…Turn, Mark thinks his name is.

Walter is the first through and he's ready – his Colt revolver is up and it's an easy adjustment to bring his arm up slightly for the correct aim.

BANG!

The shot takes the Reptilian in the head and the creature falls backward.

At nearly the same instant Bennewitz fires off a round with his gun…BOOM!...right at one of the Grays by the door.

The super soldier came next…BOOM!...and hit the other Gray at the door.

It all happened in a second or two, and then Anderholt and Carl were standing there by themselves. That didn't last long. Anderholt brought up his flash gun, pointed it at Mark still strapped there to the chair, and made to fire.

"No!" Turn shouts, and dives forward, just as the gun fires,

ZAP!

"Ugh!"

CRASH!

SLAM!

It all takes a second. Turn leaps forward and strikes the back of Mark's chair, sending them both flying toward the floor. At the same time Anderholt fires, but his shot hits the empty spot on the floor where the chair had been. Mark grunts as he hits the floor, some of the wind getting knocked out of him as Turn crashes down on top of him. And during it all Anderholt turns and makes for the door. He gets through it too, and starts down the hallway at a fast pace.

That leaves only Carl standing there, looking dumbstruck. He's unarmed, and glances nervously at the men, then down to the floor. The Reptilian's flashgun is there. Carl goes for it.

"No!" Mark shouts, both at Carl to stop going for the gun, and to the three men that'd just entered to stop them from firing. He's too late on both counts.

BANG!

A single shot from Walter's Colt takes Carl in the head and blows his blood and brains all over the metallic wall a few feet away.

"Shit," Mark says, "we coulda questioned him."

"Sorry," Walter says with a shrug.

"We're not here to take prisoners, but to free one," Bennewitz says next, rushing up to Mark and undoing his restraints, "you. Now, where's the nearest exit to this place."

Mark narrows his eyes. "What about the…" he starts to say, lifting his arm to point out the shimmering teleportation gate in their midst. As he does so, however, the gate winks out of existence.

"Uh, yeah," Bennewitz says, cocking his head to one side in a half-shrug, "we're using the teleporters from 1982."

"1982?" Mark says, and rolls his eyes as he throws his hands up in exasperation. "You know Reagan's budget cuts fucked those things up royally!"

"That's the best we could do, all things considered," Bennewitz says. "Or would you rather be dead?"

Mark only frowns to that, while Walter says, "And you still *could* be dead if we don't get the hell out of here. Now, where to?"

"Well, if we're still in Blue Lake–"

"We are," Mark says quickly.

"–then I know they'll have a time shed on a lower level."

"Then what are we standing here yappin' for?" Bennewitz says. "Let's move."

They do just that, heading out the door and into the hallway.

18 – TO THE SHED

The men burst out into the hallway. They're expecting to see guards waiting for them, guns drawn. Instead there's no one about.

"Coast's clear," Walter says.

"Let's hope it stays that way," Bennewitz adds before starting down the hall. The others follow, turning at the bend and then going down another hallway before passing by a door labeled 'stairs.'

"Gotta get down to the lower levels, the tube station levels," Mark says as he starts to push it open. No objection comes and the men start down to the lower levels of the Blue Lake base.

"I can't believe there's no one about," Turn says as they get down five flights of stairs.

"Anyone goes and checks on Mark's room and they will be," Walter says.

"Let's hope that doesn't happen in the next few–"

Before Bennewitz can finish his thought, the overhead lights switch from yellow to red, and at the end of the hallway a yellow strobe light begins to flash. A series of low 'beeping' sounds also begin, a few-second-interval between each.

"Well, guess they found Carl," Mark says with a shrug. Before anyone can answer, the low 'beeping' sound is replaced with a few bursts of static, then a voice comes across the overhead intercom system.

"Stop," it says, and right away the men recognize the voice as that of General Anderholt.

"What's he doing at Blue Lake," Bennewitz says, "…wasn't he

supposed to be at Kirtland?"

Mark shakes his head. "Came over early this morning, was at the post-mission debriefing." Mark trails-off as the voice of Anderholt comes to them again.

"Stop at once and turn yourselves in," Anderholt says, his voice loud and booming over the speaker system. "You can't get away. Turn yourselves in…there's nothing to fear."

"Yeah, *right*," Bennewitz says, rolling his eyes.

"How much further to the time shed?" Walter asks. "I'd rather not get into a shoot-out with some base guards, guards that don't know the real story about what's goin' on."

"And what *is* goin' on?" Turn asks.

"What, you haven't figured that out already?" Mark says over his shoulder, a wry smile on his face. Turn can only roll his eyes to that, though a moment later he starts down the hallway again, right after Mark starts ahead of him. "Time shed'll be on this level, and probably down this hallway…look for a door labeled 'storage room.'

"Storage room, eh?" Turn says. "And what if someone wanders in there by mistake?"

"When was the last time you saw a door labeled 'storage room' and decided to stop in for an unannounced visit?" Mark asks, to which Turn can give no response other than a slight shrug.

They continue down the hallway, the red lights on and that yellow strobe flashing. Occasionally Anderholt comes over the speakers, urging them to stop and turn themselves in to the guards that'd be appearing any moment now. They never do. Instead the men continue on for another minute, then up ahead Mark stops.

"Here it is," he says, and the others catch up and see the door labeled 'storage room." Mark reaches his hand out to open the door, but the knob won't turn. "Locked," he says, and looks at the others.

"Here," Bennewitz says, stepping forward. He reaches into his pocket and pulls out a ring of keys, flips through them for a moment, then selects one and gives it a try. The door opens with an audible 'click.'

"Where'd you get those?" Mark asks, nodding down at the keys as Bennewitz puts them back into his pocket.

"You don't wanna know," Bennewitz replies, an expressionless look on his face.

Mark shrugs to that and pushes the door open. The four men file inside, and there before them is what indeed looks like a storage room. Boxes are piled nearly up to the ceiling against one wall, while a table pushed up against another wall is also covered with them. The only thing that looks out of place is a large, rectangular box standing at one side of the room. If it wasn't for all the wires and tubes going into it, Turn would guess it was some kind of shower stall, though one without a working faucet or shower head.

"There she is," Bennewitz says, walking into the room and then over to the control panel that all the wires and tubes are leading to. It's full of buttons, many lighted red or yellow or green.

"Get her programmed for–"

Mark's words are cutoff by a shout of, "Stop, don't go any further!"

The men all turn about and look back to the door. There's no one there, but they can all hear the sound of men running down the hallway outside, their military-issued boots pounding on the cement floor.

"There's no time to program her for anything," Bennewitz says, looking back to Mark before jerking his eyes back to the controls.

"Then we'll just have to take our chances," Mark says.

"You *crazy?*" Walter says. "That time shed could lead anywhere!"

"Would you rather get into a shoot-out right here in Blue Lake?" Mark asks.

Walter frowns to that, but says nothing. Mark nods and looks back to Bennewitz. "Get 'er fired up – we're going."

Bennewitz nods, hits a few buttons on the control panel, and Turn watches as the same type of shimmering curtain of light he saw back there in Dulce appears here as well, right there in what he can only think of as a shower stall.

"Let's go!" Bennewitz shouts, and he doesn't wait for anyone to answer – he simply moves away from the controls, to that shimmering gate, and then right into it. Just like that, he's gone.

"Walter," Mark says from his spot near the door.

"You're gonna need–"

"Go," Mark says, just then sticking his head out the door.

BANG! BANG! BANG!

He pulls it back right away, the sound of gunfire echoing off the hallway walls, and looks to Walter. The captain doesn't say another word, just goes to the shimmering gate and right into it, the same as

Bennewitz had done.

"Turn, you're next," Mark says.

"Are you sure–"

"Positive," Mark says, and this time he leaves the door and comes over to stand next to Turn in front of the shimmer gate. He looks Turn in the eye, and Turn nods. Then he steps through the gate.

Behind him, Mark waits another few seconds, thinking. *How'd it all go so wrong…how'd it get to this?*

The only answer that comes are the sounds of the guards' footfalls getting closer. Mark doesn't want a fight with them – he doesn't doubt for a second that they're just doing their job, just taking orders from General Anderholt.

How deep is he in it? Mark wonders as the general crosses his thoughts. *How much does he know?*

The questions will have to wait. The footfalls are closer, just a dozen feet away now. Without another thought, Mark steps through the gate.

19 – DULCE DEPTHS

Dulce Tunnels (Level 2)
Thursday, May 24, 1979
11:45 PM

The men exit the room marked 'storage room,' leaving the time shed behind them. Turn is amazed to see that they're back in Dulce Base.

"*Here?*" he says.

"Was the last place programmed into the time shed," Bennewitz says.

"Yeah, but *why?*" Mark asks.

"And *when* are we?" Walter adds. "In case you've forgotten, we blew the hell outta this place with Stu's CED device."

"Good question," Mark says, nodding his head. "We don't want be around here when…"

The men narrow their eyes and look at Mark as he trails-off. He's got his own eyes narrowed but is looking past them. The others turn to see what he sees, and their eyes go wide.

"What the hell?" Turn says as he watches himself run by. Before anyone can answer, Andy, Johnny and then Aaron run by as well.

"We're in Dulce, and just before the place blows," Bennewitz says.

"And just before Aaron betrays us," Walter adds.

"So let's stop him!" Turn nearly shouts, nearly bolting away on his fast legs as well. A hand on his shoulder from Mark stays him, however.

"No," Mark says, shaking his head, "*that* strand of time has already run its course, and we'll let it do so again in this timeframe as well."

"Timeframe?" Turn says. "Hell, Mark – Aaron killed two of my friends back there…you think I'm just gonna let him do it again?"

"I don't think, I *know*," Mark says, a coldness in his eyes as he looks at Turn. "We didn't come here to chase after Aaron."

"Yeah, we came here to get away from Blue Lake…and didn't even know that *here* was here!" Walter says.

"But now that we *are* here," Mark says, "let's make the best of it, let's see why that time shed was set to this time, and this place."

No one argues with that, though Turn does take in a deep breath and lets it out in a slow sigh, shaking his head all the while. No one much pays attention. Instead they begin to move in the opposite way that Aaron and the others had gone. They start to…but then stop. They hear more footfalls behind them, rushing toward them this time and not away.

"Get back," Mark says, urging them up against the wall. A moment later, Aaron reappears, a bloody knife in his hand. He moves past them, far enough away and moving fast enough that he doesn't see them, and then takes a bend in the long tunnel and disappears from view.

"C'mon," Mark says, "let's see what he's up to."

"Oh, so *now* you wanna follow him, *after* he's killed Johnny again."

No one says anything to that, they just start down the tunnel. Walter is around it first, and he's just in time to see Aaron duck into a door marked 'storage room.'

"Well I'll be damned," Bennewitz says. "Bastard time-hopped outta here just before the others took off in the X-22."

"But Aaron was *on* the X-22 with me!" Mark says.

"Musta jumped out and then right back in," Walter says. "You know that with a time shed, *anything* is possible."

Mark nods to that, then looks from the door to the others. "Let's see where he goes."

"Oh, not again!" Bennewitz says. "You know how badly jumping into an unmanned time shed can turn out."

"Yeah, but we got enough time to read the display and see where it's going this time," Mark says as he starts toward the door.

The men get into the storage room and do just that, Bennewitz going up to the control panel to decipher what the light and button display is telling him. After a few moments he shakes his head, puts his hands on his hips, and turns back to them.

"Sure you wanna know?"

"Tell us," Mark says.

"Alright, but you ain't gonna like it." He shakes his head again before blurting it out. "Venus…looks like Aaron went to Venus."

"*Venus?*" Turn says.

"Only one thing's at Venus," Walter says, looking to Mark.

Mark nods. "Then let's get on board."

With that he steps into the still-shimmering gateway and disappears. After giving a few uneasy looks to one another, the other three men do the same.

20 – ON BOARD

Gray Mothership (Near Venus)
Thursday, May 24, 1979
11:55 PM

Turn comes out of the shimmering gateway and into a place he doesn't recognize. The room the four of them find themselves in looks about the same size as the room they were just in a few minutes before back at Blue Lake, though there's no chair, no Carl or Anderholt, no base guards, and certainly no aliens. *Not yet*, Turn thinks on the latter, and continues to scan his surroundings. The place certainly isn't Dulce, Turn knows. That place was strange, but not this strange. It's not that the room is *different* – it's that the whole construction and design is different. He can't recognize the metal used for the floor, or what the walls are made out of exactly. The lighting is strange, like nothing he's ever seen before. Even the door in front of them looks funny, like nothing you'd ever see on Earth.

"Welcome to space," Bennewitz says, and Turn looks up to see the wild-eyed man smiling at him.

"*Space?*"

Walter chuckles at Turn's surprise. "I imagine my face looked about the same as yours does the first time I was teleported out here."

"'Out here'…where's out here?"

"Venus, like I said back at Dulce," Mark answers, not paying attention to Turn as he checks his pockets. A moment later

Bennewitz taps him on the shoulder and hands over 9mm pistol."

"Not the sharpest tool in the box, but it'll do," he says as Mark takes the weapon.

"Venus," Turn says again, "…so what do we do and how do we get back?"

"What we do is follow Aaron," Mark says, nodding at the door. "He would have came through as the coordinates of the teleporter weren't changed."

"And what the hell's he doin' on a mothership 162 million miles from Earth, huh?" Bennewitz says.

"It's time we find out," Mark says, and moves to the door, opens it, and then after looking both ways and pulling his head in to give the others a nod, he heads through it. The others are right behind him.

They start moving down the corridors quickly, a half-jog almost.

The inside of the ship looks nothing like Turn imagined it would. The ceiling is tall, perhaps ten feet above their heads. The walls look metal but Turn can tell they're not. They're solid and almost seem to undulate, and here and there a control panel can be seen, God knows what function they have, Turn thinks. The walkways are metal. Some sections are solid while others are fence-like grates, allowing them to see down to sections below. Their booted-feet send a 'ringing' sound echoing down the corridors as they move. The lighting is dark and a faint orange, though here and there a purplish light can be seen. It's hard to make things out, and not for the first time does Turn wonder if he should put on his night vision goggles.

"Let's turn here," Bennewitz says from the front, slowing.

Behind him Walter scoffs. "Surprised you can see there *is* a turn."

"Yeah, why's it so dark?" Turn asks.

"The Grays are photosensitive," Bennewitz says in a hushed voice as he comes to a stop. He glances around the corner, seeing if it's clear. "That means any bright light hurts their eyes. They avoid sunlight like the plague and camera flashes really stun 'em." He glances around. "I can see why they like to keep this place dark."

Turn cocks his head to that in a half-shrug of understanding, and then they're moving once again. He can't believe they're not running into anyone, which in this case, he tells himself, would likely be Grays or Reptilians. *Maybe they know we're here,* he thinks*, maybe they're letting us walk right into their trap.* He pushes the thoughts away, knowing they'll do no good. And besides, he thinks, what else is he supposed to do? Not more than 12 hours ago he was killing aliens in a secret underground base. Now he's on an alien spaceship. *Maybe I'm dead already and this is all a dream.*

"Stop dreamin' and look alive," Mark says just then, drawing Turn from his thoughts. He sees that another bend in the tunnel-like hallways is up ahead, though unlike the others they've passed, there are sounds coming from the area. The men slow their pace and get up to the turn, Mark in the lead and pressing his face up against the wall. He pauses just at its edge, then after what looks like a silent prayer, he sticks his head out ever so slightly. He pulls it back a split-second later, looking up at the ceiling as if he couldn't believe what he'd just seen, or *could* believe it, but just didn't want to.

"Aaron?" Bennewitz asks, and Mark nods.

"Right around the corner, and talking with the Grays.

21 – A REAL BLOW

"I can't believe it," Mark says as he and the others watch Aaron talking with the Grays. They'd been doing so for about half a minute now, each man taking turns to move up and press his face against the wall to get the same look Mark had.

"*You* can't believe it?" Walter says. "How the hell do ya think the generals are gonna take it when *they* find out?"

"Chances are good that some of them are in on it," Mark says.

"So what do we do?" Turn asks. "How do we notify them about it? In case none of you have noticed…we're stuck on an alien spaceship of some sort, thousands of miles above the Earth!"

"Ssshhh!" several of the men make the sound, trying to quiet Turn down. Up ahead, Bennewitz looks back around the corner, sees that Aaron and the aliens are still talking, and gestures back that everything is alright.

"He's got a point," Walter says after a moment, nodding his head Turn's way, "how are we gonna–"

PING!

Walter cuts himself off as the sound of something metal hitting the craft's strange metallic floors is heard. He looks over his shoulder, as do the other men. Standing there with his face going red is Turn, and at his feet a grenade. The pin is still in it thankfully, but the small mistake of dropping it could cost them. All eyes shoot up to Bennewitz, who's just then pulling his head back from around the corner. He gives them a wide-eyed look and starts shaking his head, then is up and rushing back to them.

"They heard that!" he says in a half-shout, half-whisper as he moves past. "Aaron's already rushing for a teleporter – let's go!"

Bennewitz doesn't need to say it twice. As he shoots past the men Mark waves for the others to go too. He gets up to Turn just as he's bending down to pick up the grenade.

"Here," he says, and holds out his hand for Turn to give it over, then claps him on the shoulder and says, "go." Turn goes. Mark waits until he's a dozen feet down the hallway, then he pulls the pin on the grenade and rolls it down the hallway. It stops just a few inches from the bend in the hallway, the corner that Bennewitz had been waiting at. And with that Mark starts running. He doesn't even look over his shoulder a few moments later when a resounding 'BOOM!' can be heard.

~~~

"Go, just go!" Mark shouts ahead of him at the men rushing down the long hallway.

There are no doors, so they have to keep running. They don't know where to go, and now red lights are flashing, some sort of emergency warning system, Mark has no doubt. He knew that grenade was a mistake, even as he'd been throwing it, but what else was he supposed to do? Bennewitz said the Grays were coming, and had any of them gotten around that corner it would have been a good bet that the men would be small black piles of ash right now. Instead they were alive, though how long that would hold, Mark hadn't a clue.

The hallway continues on for another few dozen feet, then bends in another corner. The men rush around that corner and then come to a screeching halt. There before them is a small entry-port hangar of some sort. Several small UFO crafts are parked there, each levitating off the floor and swaying slightly. There are classic 'flying saucers,' craft that look V-shaped, and others that defy description. More, there's a large opening on the far wall, a clear path out of the ship and into space if there ever was one.

"There!" Mark says, pointing. "The skimmer."

"The *what?*" Turn says.

"The skimmer," Mark repeats, already breaking out into a run to the spaceship. "That's what we call 'em. They're fast and can punch into Earth orbit *real* quick." In moments the four of them are over
~~~

and standing before it.

"Can you fly that thing?" Walter asks, glancing over at Mark.

Mark just stands there for a moment with his hands on his hips before he starts rubbing at his jaw.

"Mark?" Bennewitz says.

"She's a skimmer," Mark says, more to himself than to the others, "capable of doing 650,000 miles per hour in inter-orbit bursts with booster capabilities that can put out a lot more horsepower, *a lot more.*"

"That fast and still usin' *horse*power?" Walter says, but Mark only shrugs.

"Ship like that'll take us to the moon and back in four hours, maybe less."

"But will she take us *home?*" Turn asks.

Mark looks over at him and gives a sly smile. "You bet."

"And you can fly it…right?" Walter asks again.

Mark's smile slips away and he takes on a serious expression and tone. "I could fly a bathtub if you put wings and a rudder on 'er."

"Hey, he can fly a bathtub…I feel better already."

"Can it," Walter says to Bennewitz's words, and then looks back to Mark. "So, should we–"

ZAP! ZAP! ZAP!

Walter words were cut-off as three blasts hit the wall behind the men. They look back and Turn rushes to the bend in the hallway to see what's there.

"Shit!" he says a moment later, pulling his head back and then running back to the men. "Grays, 'bout a half dozen of 'em and comin' up fast."

"Let's go," Mark says. He doesn't even wait to see if the others are coming, he just darts out toward the nearest skimmer. The others have no choice but to follow.

22 – DOGFIGHT

They get into the craft then get settled, Mark up at the controls and the others crammed into the back.

"You sure you can fly this thing?" Turn asks.

Mark scoffs and shoots him a hard look over his shoulder. "I can fly *anything*."

"Yeah, a bathtub with wings, right?" Bennewitz says. "Save that crap for the rookies – we're in deep shit here!"

"Do ya think?" Mark says in a mocking tone, but before Bennewitz can get another word in, Mark hits something and the craft launches forward. With wide eyes, the three men in the back stare out the large open window ahead of Mark. There, rushing up at them is the opening on the far wall, their pathway into space. And then they're through it, stars all around them with Earth way off in the distance.

"If we can just..." Mark says up at the controls, just before he hits something. The craft begins to move at about twice the speed it'd been going. It also enters into a continuous barrel roll.

"Oh, yeah – you can fly this thing, alright," Bennewitz says with a roll of the eyes as he clings to his seat.

"Just give me a second here..." Mark says, desperately trying to read the alien controls in front of him. He's flown all kinds of UFOs – Sirian fighter craft, Andromedan reconnaissance ships, and even a Pleiadian garbage scow once – but he's never been in a ship from the Grays. The buttons and controls all around him are in lighted colors – which is normal – but they also have strange symbols on them, which is not. Finally Mark thinks he has it figured out and slams a finger down onto one of those strange-symbol buttons.

SHOOM!

The craft speeds on in its continuous barrel rolls but now adds a loop to the mix. Soon the four men in the craft are flipping over and over to the left and right while at the same time going upside down.

"I think I'm gonna be sick," Bennewitz says, his tone dead serious for a change.

"Ah, hell," Mark says, and at that moment gives up trying to figure out what is what and just starts hitting things. Somehow he gets lucky and the craft comes out of the loop. A moment later – and another bunch of buttons pressed – and the continuous barrel rolls end. "Ha," Mark laughs, looking over his shoulder at the men behind him, "just like ridin' a bike!"

Bennewitz rolls his eyes to that. "Well then stand up on those petals and start haulin' ass – we wanna get home!"

"You can say that again," Walter adds.

"But where are we gonna go?" Turn asks. "We know Mark can't go back to Blue Lake and–"

BOOM!

Out of nowhere the craft is hit with something, lurches, and begins making sputtering sounds. Turn's words are cutoff and he and the others all look to the window in front of Mark. There's nothing there.

"What the hell was that?" Walter asks. "Felt like we just got hit with something and it sure didn't–"

BOOM!

The craft gets hit again, and this time some shrill beeping starts up, as well as what can only be a warning message of some sort, though the men don't know since it's in an alien language.

"Boys," Mark says over his shoulder, his attention on the controls and the window in front of him, "we've got company."

"Well that's just *great*!" Bennewitz says, throwing his hands up, while Turn says, "What kind of company?"

"Grays most likely, and in the same kinda crafts as us." Mark points to the small screen in front of him. "Radar's tellin' me we've got four of 'em on our tail."

"Any chance you can shake 'em?" Walter asks.

"Or turn on 'em and shoot 'em down?" Turn adds.

Mark shakes his head. "We're still 90 million miles from earth, with a rate of speed of…90,000 miles an hour."

"Damn!" Turn says from the back. "How come we haven't been ripped apart?"

"Special craft," Walter says beside him. "Built a special way so our bodies and withstand those speeds."

"Yeah," Mark says from the front, "but no way we're gonna outrun 'em."

"But we might be able to outshoot 'em, huh?" Turn asks.

"We're sure gonna find out," Mark says, then more loudly he shouts, "hang on!"

The men in the back don't get the chance to grab at anything, for Mark hits the same button that'd brought him out of the loop and is soon back in it.

"Let's see what you bastards are made of," he says under his breath to himself, and then hits another button, slowing the craft. Radar tells him what his eyes can't, and then coming out of the top of the loop, Mark sees two of their pursuers shoot past them from underneath. He hits another button and the craft regains speed, and just as a new set of warning lights and signals begin to go off.

"What's that?" Walter shouts up.

"The four on our tail are now two, but those two are *mighty* close."

"I sure hope you know what you're doin', Mark," Bennewitz says.

That makes two of us, Mark thinks, but says nothing and instead grips the control stick in front of him all the tighter. There's a button on top of it, and though Mark isn't sure what it's for, he sure hopes it does what he thinks.

"Here goes nothin'!" he says, then presses it several times.

ZAP! ZAP! ZAP! ZAP! ZAP!

A thin line of laser fire shoots out from the front of the craft. Mark uses their trails to adjust the craft's direction, firing all the while. Then he connects with one of the alien ships in front of him, hitting it first on the side where he'd normally expect a wing to be, then further into its center. One…two…three hits and it starts wobbling…four…five…*six!*

BOOM!

"Woo-hoo!" Mark shouts as the ship in front of him explodes, showering the craft next to it with debris, though not enough to damage it much or force it from the fight.

"That's one," Walter says from the back, "now just three more."

"It might help if you roll down the window and start taking pot shots at 'em with that Colt of yours," Mark says, rolling his eyes and shaking his head. That elicits a few chuckles from the men in the back, but a moment later Mark's all business again as he tries to zero-in on the craft that's still in front of him. What's more, the two behind him are now beginning to fire.

"Hang on!" Mark shouts, then pulls sharply on the controls. The skimmer goes into a spin. Outside, the laser fire from the opposing spaceship narrowly misses them.

"Oh, God…I think I'm gonna be sick!" Bennewitz says from the back.

"Better'n dead!" Mark calls back, but before anyone can get a word in he hits a few more buttons, taking them out of the loop and putting them right back into the barrel rolls. Mark also jerks the controls over to the left, taking them into a sharp turn. On his radar he can see that one of the remaining three craft is ready to zip by him. Mark jerks the controls the other way, reversing their turn, and just in time to come up right on the ship's tail.

"Abduct this, big eyes!" Mark shouts, then hits the 'fire' button once again.

ZAP! ZAP! ZAP! *BOOM!*

Two misses and then the third shot landed just right. The alien ship simply explodes in a fiery ball.

"Two left," Mark calls back. "Now we just gotta–"

BOOM!

Mark's words are cutoff as they're hit. Loud beeping begins to sound, just as the interior lights in the craft switch from their faint yellow to a dangerous red. Mark looks around with wide eyes, and just as their craft begins to flounder and fall, losing altitude as well as control.

"Uh, Mark…please tell me we're alright," Bennewitz calls up from the back.

"We're alright!" Mark shouts back, wishing that was the case. The control panel is telling him that his speed has dropped about 100,000 miles while radar is telling him that the last two craft are lining up behind him, coming in for the kill. Besides that their stolen ship seems to be doing alright, despite the hit they've just taken. Mark begins to think fast, his countless hours of training in various fighter craft on Earth and off-world coming back to him. He gets an idea.

"Boys, you might want to hold on back there…things are gonna get *real* bumpy here, and *real* fast."

There are some groans to that, mainly from Bennewitz, but the three men in the back say nothing, just grab their seats and hope for the best. Mark hopes too. Looking at the controls he knows he's at a serious disadvantage. He can't match the aliens' speed nor their fast moves, not after taking that hit. One more like it an he's sure they'll be out of the fight, if not blown apart entirely. So Mark flips through his mental notebook of aerial combat maneuvers, and finally settles on the only option he really has – the scissors.

The move is quite simple, really, and one that Mark pulled off countless times in Vietnam…even though the move was frowned upon then, and had been ever since the Korean War days. It just wasn't adequate anymore with the advanced fighters and the various thrust-to-weight ratios and wing loading that made it almost a given that anyone trying the scissors maneuver would be shot down. But Mark figured the aliens he was fighting didn't know that, and had never seen the move. Well, he was hoping that was the case, and started into it.

Continuing on in the barrel roll, mark started the move for the rolling scissors. With one of the alien fighter craft on top of him now, and the other one not too far behind, Mark began to roll in such a way that one second the alien was on top of him, then two seconds later below him. It was that second in between that counted, that brief moment when the two craft were lined up. The problem was that currently they were side-to-side. Mark knew he had to get behind that alien craft, if only a little bit. To do that Mark initiates a pull-up into vertical, causing the alien ship to overshoot him a bit and pull ahead. Mark then rolls his craft, increasing the speed of separation for a brief moment. Now the alien fighter is ahead of him further, and just enough, he hopes. Glancing at the radar, Mark can see the other alien fighter is right behind him…and about to lock on.

"Here goes," Mark says quietly, and then pulls the kicker.

He pulls the controls and the craft goes into a snap roll, allowing the fighter ahead of Mark to move ahead further. Still moving nearly parallel to each other in their barrel rolls, the alien ship is now slightly ahead. Mark continues in the rolls.

"Wait for it…wait for it…wait for…" he says to himself, then fires.

ZAP! ZAP! ZAP! ZAP! ZAP! BOOM!

It takes several shots but finally one connects and the fighter craft begins to lose altitude. Mark doesn't wait to watch it but immediately pulls back on the controls, entering into a loop. The warning controls begin chirping violently, for a collision is imminent. Mark knows this, knows the alien fighter on his tail will hit him if it doesn't disengage and break off. And it does, pulling away while Mark continues his loop. Then when he comes out of it, the fighter is right there in front of him, now desperately trying to dodge out of the way. Mark fires.

ZAP! ZAP! ZAP! *BOOM!*

The fighter is hit on the third shot, though it's just a grazing shot. Still, it's enough to send the craft hurtling, and at a very high rate of speed. It flies forward right at the other alien fighter, the one that Mark just hit in his scissors move. Then it hits, bounces off, and both craft begin hurtling, one rolling and pitching in a very unnatural way. Judging by its speed, Mark figures any Grays inside of it have been smashed apart against the craft's inside walls. He watches both ships hurtle away, knowing that if they were on Earth the ships would be falling toward the ground to crash. There was no ground out here in space, but there was still gravity. It was caused by the pull of Venus, and both craft got locked into it. They slowly pull toward the planet, and Mark and the others watch for a minute as they increase in speed as the atmosphere takes them. Then they begin to change color, going from the silver-metallic-black to a reddish-orange-yellow as the heat of the atmosphere takes them. The glowing increases in intensity and then – poof! – the craft are on fire, then disintegrating.

"Good riddance," Walter says from the back, and the others nod to that.

"Now, how 'bout gettin' us home!" Bennewitz calls up.

Mark smiles. "You got it."

23 – SAFE HARBOR

Somewhere over the Pacific Ocean
Friday, May 25, 1979
3:00 PM

After hours of flying through space, Mark finally steers the skimmer into Earth's orbit. After heating up to 3,000 degrees Fahrenheit it reenters the Earth's atmosphere and a few moments later the four of them are cruising through the clouds.

"Where are we?" Walter calls up from the back.

"Right now? About 2,000 miles west of the Oregon Coast." Mark looks at some of the console readouts as he speaks. "Should be coming up on dry land again in fifteen minutes or so."

"And where to then?" Turn asks next.

"A safe place," Mark replies.

"Oh?" Bennewitz says next. "Mind filling us in on what that might be?

"It's an old port in Montana," Mark replies."

"*Montana* again," Turn says, "what the hell?

"Uh…yeah, Mark," Walter says, "what's with that place? It's up in the middle of nowhere…probably got more cows than people."

"You're right on both fronts," Mark says, "and that's exactly why the government likes to put secret stuff there…stuff they don't want anyone else to know about." He shrugs. "Montana's a good spot – mostly mountains and forests to block and cover things, hardly anyone around to go prying about."

"So it's back to that place around Hopland, then?" Walter asks.

"God, no," Mark says, his face screwing up. "We go back there and the traitors at Blue Lake'll know it in a heartbeat."

"But…that was a place full of Grays," Turn says.

Bennewitz chuckles. "But remember, the Grays are still working with the highest levels of our government, just as they have been since Eisenhower signed the treaty."

"And even before," Mark adds.

"So if not Hopland then where?"

"Place north of the capital city a ways, right beside a lake," Mark says as he turns the craft more to the west, "an old UFO crashed there back in the 1860s, even got some press as far south as St. Louis."

"Damn, the *1860s*?" Walter says. "I'm surprised anyone was around back then to know about it."

"Fur trapper saw her come down," Mark says. "He went in to investigate and figured it was a big space rock or something. Remember, there were no airplanes back then."

"So what happened?" Turn asks.

"Nothing…at least at first. The trapper headed off to wherever, the locals in the area didn't much care – Montana wasn't a state yet – and no one 2,000 miles south in St. Louis gave a damn, either. So the crashed UFO sat there."

"How long?"

"More than 20 years, until deep into the 1880s. That's when a Utah & Northern Railroad company team building a line through the area discovered it. Word got back to investors, then to the feds. It was hushed up, the craft was studied, and it was agreed they'd build an underground base there, under the guise of the railroad, of course. Base lasted until into the 1920s, when post-World War I cuts forced its closure. By that time the company that'd started it was off to bigger and better things." Mark laughs. "Can anyone guess their name?" Silence, and Mark laughs again. "Why, Bechtel, of course."

"The same that built Dulce," Bennewitz says.

"Exactly," Mark replies.

A silence falls after that, and the men settle down to looking out the windows. After another ten minutes Mark is telling them they're making their approach. Pine, spruce and fir trees pass by the windows, none rising higher than the rocky mountains all around them. Then with a 'screech' the craft touches down, though that's not quite accurate, as its levitation powers keep it a couple feet off the ground.

"Welcome to Montana," Mark says, and pops the door on the skimmer.

PART V

24 – FIGHTING BACK

Blue Lake
Friday, May 25, 1979
3:17 PM

Bobbie turns yet another hallway in the large Blue Lake base, and once again he curses under his breath. Charlie isn't there, just as he hasn't been in any of the half dozen hallways that Bobbie has run down already. He has to find him, too, he has to tell him what he suspects. Chargin' Charlie is about the only one he thinks he can trust right now, well, besides Donlon.

And I might as well not go to him as he'd just have to go to Charlie anyways, the super soldier thinks as he continues down the hallway. While their official military rank might not mean a lot on the special alien-busting teams they've found themselves on, there's still an unwritten level of seniority within the teams. Bobbie knows that, Donlon knows that, and Charlie knows that. So Bobbie keeps racing down the hallway, hoping that around the next turn he'll finally see…

"Charlie!" Bobbie blurts out as he rounds the next corner and finally sees the colonel. He's walking with a base guard, going over a clipboard by the looks of it. At the sight of Bobbie he looks up, gives a nod and says something to the guard, and then hands the clipboard over before signing off on the bottom of it. By the time Bobbie has raced down the hallway to him, the guard is gone and Charlie is standing there with his arms crossed, an impatient look on his face.

"What'dya need, Bobbie?"

"Something's going on, sir."

"Yeah, something's goin' on alright – besides the chaos over Mark and Ellis this morning I've got two pallets o' grenades and another of shoulder-fired rockets and can't find room in storage to put either of 'em!" He shakes his head, giving out a resigned, "Shit!" as he does so.

Bobbie narrows his eyes, not sure what to say to that, so he just says it. "Listen, man…I don't know where Jake went."

"*Don't know…*" Charlie starts to repeat, then Bobbie's tone gets to him and he frowns and narrows his eyes instead. "Listen, *man*…it's a big base, and there's a lot of *work* to do…ever try any?"

Bobbie rolls his eyes to that. "Sir, I'm telling you – there's something going on here!"

"Yeah, the only thing that's going on is that you're wasting my time, and worse, you're wasting…"

Charlie trails-off and narrows his eyes as something coming down the hallway gets his attention. Bobbie narrows his eyes too and turns around to look. There coming toward them is a beautiful young woman, blond hair flowing well past her shoulders. Neither man thinks they've ever seen a flight suit looking so good.

She continues down the hall toward them, her eyes locked on Charlie. Both men stand back, in awe of her beauty, and a bit taken aback by her confident stride. Finally she gets there.

"You're Chargin' Charlie, right?"

"Yes ma'am, ,er…I mean, miss."

Bobbie looks over and sees Charlie's face going a bit red. He might have been one tough hombre back in Vietnam and wherever else he waged war, but get a beautiful woman in front of him and it was clear his knees started turning to jelly.

"I need to talk with you," she says to him, glancing over at Bobbie then back at him, "*alone*."

"Well, I…uh…sure, I mean…"

Bobbie gives a quick glance over at Charlie mumbling to himself, he rolls his eyes and shakes his head a bit, and then takes a step forward.

"What's this all about, Heather?" he says, then, "That is your name, right – Heather? Your Mark's old flame."

"Old flame, eh? He tell you that."

"No," Bobbie says, growing a bit flustered, "I just put two and two together after seeing both of you."

Heather gives him a skeptical look. "Sounds like you need to work on your math. *Anyways*," she says, turning back to Charlie, who's now looking a bit more flustered than Bobbie suddenly does, "if you're Charlie – and I imagine you must be, as no one else is gonna look like the butcher in *Marty* – then you're probably the only person on this whole base that I can trust right now."

"Whoa, wait a minute there, miss…what the hell's goin' on here, and don't mind Bobbie here – might look dumb, but he's quite harmless despite that, let me assure you."

Heather glances Bobbie's way, raises her brows for a moment in a way that makes the super soldier feel both hopeful and worthless at the same time, and then looks back to Charlie.

"Alright," she says, brushing some of that blond hair out of her eyes, "I guess it's gonna take more than just me and you anyways, so we might as well figure out who we can trust, because after what I've seen today, I'm not sure the people I've known for *years* are even on my side anymore."

"Heather, what's going on?" Bobbie asks, putting his hands on his hips and taking on his best 'serious' expression.

"Yeah," Charlie echoes, "we'd love to help ya – especially if it's got something to do with the Dutchman or his son – but we *gotta* know what's going on first."

Heather looks from Charlie to Bobbie and back again, then to the floor before letting out a big sigh. *Here it goes*, she thinks.

"General Anderholt is working with the Reptilians and even ordering about some Grays," she blurts out. *He's* the one that killed Jake, though it was Carl that killed Ellis and framed Mark."

"*What?*" both men blurt out at the same time, though Bobbie adds a, "How do you *know* all this?"

"Long story," Heather says – something Bobbie thinks is probably the most believable thing she's said yet, while Charlie says, "Well, you better get ready to tell it."

"I will," Heather replies, glancing about, "but not here."

"I know somewhere safe," Charlie says, then with a shrug of his brows, "or at least, I *thought* I did until running into you just now." He quickly adds, "And that's not to say I *believe* all o' what I'm hearing here, either."

"Just give me a chance to tell it," Heather replies.

Charlie nods and glances at Bobbie. “Go find Donlon and meet me in the east hangar in five minutes.”

“Yes, sir,” Bobbie says, and races off down the hallway.

25 – THEIR MASTER PLAN

The Gates of the Mountains north of Helena, Montana
Friday, May 25, 1979
3:32 PM

The men file into the old Montana base, tiredness sapping their movements. It'd been a long day and night for all of them, and rest was sought after the most. Information was a close second.

"Before we go too much farther," Turn says, plopping down in one of the chairs in a large meeting room off the hangar, "will someone please tell me what the hell's goin' on here…and I don't just mean a brief synopsis, either. I want to know it *all!*"

Bennewitz looks to Mark and then the others before settling back on Mark. "He's come this far…he deserves to know."

Mark glances down at his watch. "*All*, you say? Not sure if we have time for all that, but we just might be able to get most of it."

Walter chuckles. "Good luck with that. Or were you *not* going to go all the way back to the dinosaurs?"

"*Dinosaurs?"* Turn says, his face screwing up, although he thinks, *maybe it's not too far-fetched…if that's what they're getting at. I mean, dinosaurs are lizards, and Reptilians are lizards, and…*

Turn lets those thoughts trail-off, feeling even more confused than ever. Mark seems to read that expression.

"Oh, boy…where to begin?" he says.

"How 'bout from the top?" Bennewitz says with a laugh.

"Alright," Marks says, cocking his head, "here goes." He starts pacing across the room, then a few moments later launches into it. "It all started with the Reptilian invasion of Lyra millennia ago. Initially there were negotiations, but in the end the Lyran system was devastated, with three planets destroyed. This started the human diaspora throughout the galaxy. Eventually we humans settled in 110 different star systems, including the Pleiades and Alpha Centauri." He shrugs. "Today most of those 110 human races are part of the Star Federation, or what we usually just call the Collective."

"You see, Turn," Bennewitz says, "Humans didn't start here on Earth, but at Lyra…the harp-shaped constellation that's 25 light years from us."

"And the Reptilians started at Draco," Mark says, taking the tale up once again. "No one's really sure when, but an old Apache Indian from the Dulce area named Robert Morning Sky has an idea. He was given esoteric information from his grandfather about the origins of the Reptilians, information that's been passed down through the years. Supposedly an alien craft crashed on the reservation, there was one alien survivor named Bkti, and a group of six Indian men found him and nursed him back to health. That was more than a century ago yet that's how our information on the origins of the earth and the alien societies in contact with us was first learned."

"A lot to swallow, I know," Bennewitz says, seeing the look on Turn's face.

Mark nods to that before continuing. "Supposedly their race appeared in Draco millions of years ago, and its even speculated that they might have come from another dimension or time frame before that. Morning Sky thinks they developed and evolved from dragonflies." Mark shrugs. "On their own planet the males do have wings…so it's possible." He shrugs again. "What we *can* be sure of is that humans started off around the same time, though down a much different path of enlightenment.

"What you have to understand," Walter says, "*we* have souls, the Grays and the Reptilians do not. Yet they crave that higher-level energy that our souls give us, want it for their own. So they steal it, and they've been doing so for a very long time."

Mark nods. "They're a warlike race and they live to fight and conquer. They're smart too, though, and take the resources from the places they conquer, whether it's what's under the ground or what's in the bodies of those living atop it…that soul energy that Walter is getting at."

"*Whew!*" Turn says with a whistle. "That's a lot to digest."

"I know," Mark says, "I couldn't believe it all the first time I heard it either. Anyways, the Reptilians started by enslaving conquered societies, but learned that didn't work too well in the long-run…too much resistance. So over time they started using a banking system that required the contribution of large amounts of resources to a central bank that they controlled."

"Sound familiar?" Walter says. "They've foisted the same system onto us over the centuries, whether it's the Fugger or De Medicis in Italy, the Vatican Bank later on, or our own three national banks here in America, the latest of which we call the Federal Reserve."

Turn nods, not so much because he understands it all, but just to let the men know he's hearing them, and trying to process it.

"So the Reptilians destroy our ancestral system and we humans flee across the universe," Mark says, picking up the story again. "Draco is 148 light years from Earth, a much greater distance than the 25 light years Lyra is. We thought we'd be safe here…but we were wrong." Mark lets out a sigh at this point, rubs his forehead for a moment, then starts again. "We humans reached the Milky Way Galaxy and settled on Mars, as well as another planet called Maldech. At that point Maldech was the third planet from the sun. That situation lasted for millions of years before the Reptilians found us."

"But…I thought you said we were too far away."

"For a spaceship, maybe, but the Reptilians didn't come in a spaceship…they came in a planet."

Turn takes on a strange look at that, and Walter claps him on the shoulder. "Bit much, ain't it?"

"You can say that again."

Mark smiles, remembering when he'd heard it all. He hadn't looked much different. He decides to keep going. "It didn't take long before Maldech was destroyed. Today its remnants make up our asteroid belt. They also stripped the atmosphere from Mars, forcing the Martian humans underground. It was the only way they could survive."

"At that point," Bennewitz says, "many humans came to Earth. It wasn't what it is today, however. It was a water planet, totally covered. They had to use technology to dry the place out, evaporating all that water up into the atmosphere so that the planet was habitable. The moon was also created so that life could be sustained."

"Created?" Turn says, his face screwing up in confusion.

"Yeah," Mark says with a laugh, "it ain't cheese but it *is* made of metal. She doesn't rotate, either, just faces in that one direction." He takes in a deep breath. "Anyways, the Reptilians weren't going to let us get away that easy. They chased us right here to Earth, and settled down on the planet as well. They even brought their own flora and fauna. That includes the dinosaurs, which was their food source."

"Don't believe it?" Walter says. "Check the fossil record – there's nothing those beasts could have evolved from…they just appeared."

"It didn't take long for the Collective to learn of this pestering so far from them. They got tired of the Reptilians on Earth and sent the Atlanteans here. They colonized the continent of Atlantis. This was a fierce race, one that'd been from Lyra and had fought hard against the Reptilians. After Lyra was destroyed they moved to the Pleiades, but their fighting spirit caused too much trouble. That's when they were sent to Earth, to both get rid of them and to pit them against the Reptilians. They were able to sink the continent of Lemuria – which was the 6,000-mile wide continent where the Reptilians had settled, and sometimes called simply 'Mu' - thus forcing the aliens underground. That was 300,000 years ago and they've been there ever since. They didn't go without a fight, though, and they haven't stopped fighting since they've been down there. It took them awhile, but they tinkered enough with the large belt of natural gas under Atlantis so that it became over-compressed, sinking the continent. That threw Earth into a deep and prolonged dark age, one that lasted for millennia. The fighting never really stopped, however, though by 50,000 years ago it'd heated up again. This led to the nuclear war over what's now India, culminating in the war's end around the year 2600 BC. Since then it's been quiet, with the 2,000 or so Reptilians that are left mostly focused under the Indian subcontinent and in Antarctica."

"Just 2,000 of 'em?" Turn says. "You've got to be kidding me!"

"I'm not," Mark says, "those are their numbers."

Bennewitz chuckles. "Not many, eh? Well trust me – they're damn hard to get rid of when they dig themselves in, like they've done here."

"They've never been good at reproducing, hence their reliance on the Grays as workers and underlings," Mark says. "It's one of the drawbacks of not having a soul – you can't make new souls. They hate that, and despise anyone that has that ability over them."

"It's one of the reasons they go out into the universe and conquer and enslave," Walter says.

"They've conquered and enslaved 21 other star systems, taking over the levers of power from within," Mark says. "They use spies and then hybridize the surface population. This is their fifth column and we hardly stand a chance against it. In many ways – like with the Illuminati – we've already been defeated."

Bennewitz nods to that. "The threat they pose from without – and the threat the humans working with them pose from within – makes them nearly impossible to defeat."

"But we can do it…right?" Turn says.

"Humanity's depending on us," Mark says.

"Depending on us to root out the traitors," Walter says.

"It all comes back to the military cabal that's associating with the Reptilians," Bennewitz says. "We know that 13,000 children have been taken by the Reptilians over the past 25 years."

"Why?" Turn asks.

"They drink the blood, and they prefer the blood of humans that's unpolluted. When adults, the blood is usually polluted with all *kinds* of things. So they take the children."

"Wasn't always like that," Bennewitz continues. "When the dinosaurs were destroyed they began to use the humans as their main food source. So this has been going on for as long as human history."

"I just can't believe it," Turn says.

"Better start," Mark replies. "Thousands of humans disappear each year all over the world, and most of them can be chalked-up to the Grays doing the abducting, the Reptilians doing the eating. They have to. You see, the blood contains the life force, which is what they live on. They live in the fourth dimension, a lower astral realm, and to manifest in the third dimension they need the energy of human blood and human flesh."

"God…can we even stop 'em?"

Mark nods. "The path to victory is through expanding our consciousness, for at that point they can no longer affect us *or* control us. And when you get right down to it, the Reptilians are afraid of us. That's why they seek to control us. They know that when *our* consciousness expands, they'll be done here."

"And that's why they're fighting all the harder now," Bennewitz says, "that's why they've infiltrated our society, pitting the haves against the have-nots. And they *always* seek out the most evil among us."

"Like Hitler," Mark says, looking to Turn. "It's not taught in school, but the Nazis created the current underground Antarctic colony way back in 1938, and they did so at the invitation of the Reptilians."

"Ha!" Bennewitz laughs. "*That* didn't work out too well for 'em."

"No, Hitler probably wasn't the best choice," Mark admits. "Reptilians have problems controlling the human race, and Hitler is a prime example why. They can't control the kind of madness that often takes hold in leaders, like it took hold in that nutcase. At that point the Reptilians have no use for them."

"But…why work with them at all?" Turn asks.

"Simple – greed and power," Bennewitz replies. "The Reptilians control the planet through the secret society called the Illuminati, who in turn control the banks, the media and the pharmaceutical companies. Those corrupt systems have been in place for decades, and in some cases centuries."

"But there's more to it than that," Mark says. "Those that are the most loyal will be 'rewarded' with Reptilian blood of their own." He shrugs. "It's powerful stuff. Reptilians learned to shape shift a *long* time ago, and that can be passed on to the hybrid Reptilian/human combinations. However, this can *only* be done if the hybrids have 45% Reptilian blood or more." He scoffs. "And trust me – there are a *lot* of half-Reptilian, half-humans running around."

"We call them 'blue bloods' as they have a lot of copper in their blood, or a what can be considered a large percentage of Reptilian blood," Bennewitz says. "Many, many leaders throughout history have had it. Take the Emperor of Japan, Hirohito. He got his Reptilian blood from the Imoto clan, and going back to the 16th century. Maybe he's even a shape shifter."

"We know Queen Elizabeth is one," Mark says.

"Oh, now you've *got* to be joking," Turn says.

"Wish I was," Mark says, shrugging. "The bottom line is that it's easier to influence humanity directly this way, with hybrids in charge of nations. Remember, Reptilians are in the minority on this planet, always have been, and by a *very* wide margin."

"Yeah, just 2,000, right?" Turn says, and Mark nods.

"Hardly any, but with their chimera-robot-like Grays doing most of the work for them they get the job done, and *have* been getting it done for thousands of years."

"They control us, Turn," Bennewitz cuts in, "always have and always will…unless we do something about it."

"And now's the time to do it," Mark says, pounding a fist into the palm of his hand." He then looks to Turn. "It's also time to tell you who you really are, Turn, and where you really come from…or as I should say, *when* you really come from."

26 – A FRIEND INDEED

Blue Lake
Friday, May 25, 1979
3:38 PM

Five minutes after leaving Charlie to race down the hallway, Bobbie comes rushing into the east hangar, Colonel Roger Donlon in tow. Waiting there for them are Charlie and Heather. Charlie glances down at his watch before looking up at Bobbie.

"What happened to five minutes, eh?"

Bobbie shrugs. "You try racin' all the way to the *west* hangar and back in that time."

"Well, you're here now," Charlie says, "so let's get down to it."

"Bobbie filled me in on the way over," Donlon says. He's a crew-cut military man, brass on the chest and a no-nonsense look on his face. He directs that look at Charlie. "I have to admit, I was having doubts already. I'm glad I'm not the only one."

Charlie was just about to speak up when a 'fwapping' sound suddenly starts up in the hallway. It's faint, but growing in volume.

"Someone's coming!" Heather says.

"But who can know?" Bobbie says.

The four find out a moment later when the 'fwapping' sound ends and the door flies open. Standing there is Stu.

"Stu, what the hell are *you* doin' here!" Charlie nearly shouts.

"I've got to get to Montana," Stu says.

Heather narrows her eyes to that. "What's going on?"

"The Trifecta – it's started."

"*Already?*" she says, and Stu nods. "You'll never believe who told me all about it."

"Oh, I have some ideas," Heather replies.

"Um…can someone tell me what the hell's goin' on here?" Donlon says after a moment.

"Yeah, we're having a meeting about what the hell we're supposed to be doing…and now we've got Stu here mucking it all up."

"Sorry," Stu says, holding up his hands defensively.

Charlie just shakes his head and looks back to Donlon. "Anyways, you said you were having doubts? And what doubts might those be?"

"'Bout Anderholt, mostly." As Donlon says the words he thinks back to the night before, and their raid on Dulce. "A call came in from General Anderholt on the satellite radio, but not until the train of women captives had nearly filled up." He shrugs, looking down at the floor. "I remember thinking that it was almost like the general had a camera and was *watching* us." He looks back up at Charlie. "I shook the thought off at the time as another train began to come in, but it's been nagging at me ever since."

"Something's always bothered me about that ol' dinosaur Anderholt," Charlie says, shaking his head and looking off for a moment before turning his attention back to the others. "You know he was the first to discover Dulce, right? Or at least the first military men to get the Indians to lead him to it."

"I didn't know that," Donlon says. "I knew he was one of the first that was involved, but…well, what about the Indian legends?"

Charlie shrugs. "Beats me."

"Guys, I think we're getting a little ahead of ourselves," Heather says. "Remember, Mark is gone…and Carl is dead. Things like that don't just happen, not on a military base like this one. So…are you thinking what I'm thinking?"

"You betcha," Charlie says, then looks to Donlon. "Bennewitz is involved."

"Oh, *hell!*" Donlon says with a frown, putting his hands on his hips to pace around a bit.

"*Bennewitz?*" Bobbie says. "Who the hell's that?"

"Paul Bennewitz," Heather answers. "He was one of the first to discover Dulce and the alien connection, way back in the day. It wasn't until the 80s though that he *really* got involved, and by 'really' I mean with John Titor and the 177th."

"Um…*80s?"* Bobbie says, his face screwing up as if Heather had just started speaking a foreign language to him.

"The 1980s," Stu says, then looks to Charlie. "We can spend a lot of time rehashing and explaining, or we can just send him to Montana with me."

"Do you really think they're up there?" Charlie says.

"That's the plan, always has been," Heather answers. "Besides, Stu here said that's where he needs to go."

"You can kinda say I told myself," Stu says.

Donlon rolls his eyes. "*Time travel!* God, I'll never get used to it!"

"Whoa…Montana again?" Bobbie says, putting his hands up. "And what the hell's all this about the 1980s, huh? That decade is still six months off! And time travel? *Shit!"*

Everyone ignores Bobbie, and Heather continues talking, much to the super soldier's exasperation.

"And if they're in Montana then it's a good bet they'll be going for the Trifecta, just like Stu here says."

"The…*Trifecta?"* Bobbie manages to get in.

Donlon nods. "That's the unofficial name for the three-part plan that the Dutchman came up with years ago, when we first started trying to take Dulce back."

"God, he was *serious* about that?" Charlie says, his face screwing up as he looks from Donlon to the others and back again.

"Deathly serious," Donlon replies.

"So how's the plan go?" Heather asks.

"Yeah, how's it go?" Bobbie adds.

"Well," Donlon starts, cocking his head to one side in a half-shrug, "it might sound far-fetched…but here goes. The first part involves taking down the Gray's soul catcher, an advanced machine that acts like a net around the Earth, capturing human souls as they leave their bodies and head for the afterlife."

"You've *got* to be kidding," Bobbie says.

"The second part," Donlon continues, shrugging his brows at Bobbie's comment but nothing more, "involves the alien base on the dark side of the moon."

"I thought we took that out," Stu says.

Donlon shakes his head. "Not in this timeline. We took it out once, but the Grays initiated a time-shift and that reality was wiped clean, or at the very least cut off to us."

"Kinda like the Lake Oswego Incident," Charlie says, and Donlon nods.

"And the third part of the plan?" Bobbie says, then holds up his hand. "Wait…let me guess – taking out Hitler before he has a chance to flee Germany and head to…where, exactly…South America…*Antarctica?*"

Donlon narrows his eyes and gives Bobbie a strange, but serious, look. "You sure this is all new to you?"

"Oh, you've got to be kidding!" Bobbie says, throwing up his hands and pacing about a bit.

"Well, Hitler and Antarctica is an entirely different story, and one that's not the third part of the Dutchman's Trifecta. What *is* the third part of it, however, is a crashed UFO that we know of from the 177th's time in the future."

"Titor again, eh?" Charlie says, and Donlon nods.

"Report he filed from 2031 tells us that the Russian crash is a *lot* more important than we realized…or realize…or – hell, you know what I mean!"

Heather chuckles. "Always hard keepin' track of things when time travel's involved, isn't it?"

"You can say that again," Donlon says with a smile, then looks to the others once more, his serious tone back. "Anyways, if Mark is indeed going to try for the Trifecta then he'll need our help…*and* the knowledge that we're aware of what he's doing, and are there for him."

"And how the hell's he gonna learn that, huh?" Bobbie says.

"By sending us there to tell him," Stu says, then looks to Donlon. "We can still rev up the teleporter in the basement, right?"

Donlon shrugs. "You mean after we dust the cobwebs off? I hope so."

"Um…guys..." Bobbie says, "…teleporter…*cobwebs?*"

"Don't worry," Heather says, coming over to clap him on the shoulder, "it's a lot worse than it sounds."

27 – BARGING IN

The Gates of the Mountains north of Helena, Montana
Friday, May 25, 1979
3:44 PM

"When you really come from?" Turn thinks to himself, repeating the phrase over and over in his mind that Mark just said out loud. He's just about to throw out his first question – a sarcastic one at that – but before he's able to do so a strange feeling overtakes him. It feels like…static electricity. Narrowing his eyes, Turn looks around and sees that others are taking on strange looks as well, as if they too notice.

"Feel that?" Walter is the first to say.

"Static, and building fast," Bennewitz says, and right when the words are out of his mouth he looks to Mark. Both men speak at the same time.

"Someone's comin' in!"

"Someone…?" Walter manages, but trails-off as the static build-up in the air increases, and then electrical sparks begin to appear. They're like miniature lightning bolts, blue and flashing here and there. The lights in the room begin to dim, and then a crackling sound can be heard.

"Look out!" Mark shouts, and just as he begins to dive for the wall. He's not a second too late – just then a shimmering portal appears in the middle of the room, the same kind that Turn saw back in Dulce just hours before. It stands there flickering that oil-in-apuddle look for a moment, and then there's a bright flash as someone comes through. And then just like that the portal is gone. It takes a moment for the four men in the room to adjust their eyes, but when they do they widen them in surprise.

"Bobbie!" Turn is the first to say, followed by a, "Stu!" from Walter and a, "What in the hell are *you two* doing here?" from Mark.

"Hey, it's nice to see you too!" Bobbie says in that go-fuck-yourself tone of his.

"No, I'm serious," Mark says, "what are you doing here? What's happened at Blue Lake?"

"What…you don't know?" Stu says. "Gosh, you sent me back from here to tell me to get ready, and come here now!"

"Don't know?" Bobbie scoffs. "Course they know. Or were you thinking of something else besides your father gettin' killed and you takin' the blame before breakin' yourself out?" Bobbie shrugs. "Not a whole lot."

"Something's happened or you two wouldn't have been sent here," Walter says.

"Yeah, somethin's happened alright," Bobbie says. "Carl was killed in that breakout of yours and people are beginning to wonder. One of 'em was Jake, and when he took his concerns to General Anderholt…well, he vanished."

"*Vanished?*" Bennewitz says. "Or maybe just went AWOL? I hear there's a mighty fine bar just a couple miles from Blue Lake, after all."

Bobbie chuckles. "And I could clean out their full stock right about now. "No," he continues, shaking his head, "Jake wouldn't have run off like that…something's happened to him. And when you couple that somethin' with the Dutchman's death and you takin' the blame for it, well…" he looks at Mark and nods as he says that last, "then there's a pretty good bet that something's going on, and it sure ain't good."

"So you found Donlon and he told you about the plan," Mark says.

"If you mean the Trifecta, then yes." Bobbie shrugs, looking from Mark to Walter to Turn and finally at Bennewitz. "Donlon thought you'd be here. Said you might have some strange company too."

"Strange as in new and different…or strange as in something else?" Bennewitz says, getting up close to the super soldier and looking at him this way and that. Bobbie begins to grow uncomfortable, like he's suddenly some zoo animal.

"Uh…just strange," Bobbie says.

"And of course my future self told me…and now he's…where exactly?" Stu says.

"Waiting to turn into you," Mark says, giving Stu a strange look. "Didn't you write the book on the physics of time travel, after all?"

Stu only frowns to that.

"If we sent you back then that means you're going after Tommy," Bennewitz says, "and that means the soul catcher's days are numbered."

Stu rolls his eyes. "I was afraid it was something like that."

Bobbie takes the slight lull in the conversation to look back at Mark. "Say, what the hell *is* goin' on around here? And this is Montana…right? Donlon said you'd probably be in Montana…right before he stuck me in that teleporter gizmo and sent me here."

"Yep, this is Montana," Mark says, "and Donlon was right about where we'd head. But I'm troubled to hear it's mainly business as usual back at Blue Lake. Are you telling me that's it…that no one's doubting the bullshit Anderholt's feedin' em?"

Bobbie shakes his head. "Besides Donlon and Charlie and Heather and me–"

"Heather!" Mark says, rushing forth to grasp hold of Bobbie's shoulders. "Is she alright? Anderholt hasn't gotten to her?"

"No…no!" Bobbie says, surprised at the vehemence in Mark's voice. "She's fine…and working with us…and by 'us' I mean Charlie and Donlon and me."

"That's it?" Bennewitz says.

Bobbie scoffs. "What the hell'd you expect…the cavalry? C'mon, pal – can't you see what's goin' on? It's sure clear to me at least that we've got traitors in our midst, and they're probably working with the Grays."

"And the Grays have always worked for the Reptilians," Mark says, more to himself than anyone else. He looks lost in thought. The others see this and leave him to it.

The men – now numbering six instead of four – get settled back down. A moment of looking about comes, as if they're trying to remember what it was they were discussing before everything got thrown off by Bobbie and Stu's unexpected entrance. Finally Mark clears his throat, pulling all eyes to him. He in turn looks to Turn.

"Like I was sayin' before these two jumped in us…let's explain where you *really* come from."

28 – OLD MEMORIES

Turn scoffs. "Where I *really* come from? C'mon, Mark – maybe you've been in space too long."

Mark ignores the doubt and launches into the explanation. He knows from past experience that this is the best way to do it, the best way to bring a man's memories back. *Slow and easy*, Mark tells himself, *slow and easy.*

"The idea all along was to have a program that takes veterans of *future* wars and uses them to make the super soldiers of today…or the past, if that's how you want to look at it." Mark looks to Turn. "That's how you came to be in 1979, Turn."

"*What?*" Turn says, giving him a narrow-eyed, suspicious look that said, *'you're full of shit!'*

"It's true," Mark continues, looking from Turn to the others, "the favorite right 'now' is to take veterans from the wars in Iraq and Afghanistan that are 'currently' being fought in the 2000s and 2010s." He looked back to Turn. "My father showed me your file before he died. General Anderholt recruited you from your hospital bed in 2003…just days after you'd had your legs blown off in the Iraqi city of Fallujah."

"They were blown off in some alley in Cambodia!" Turn says, growing perturbed at how the conversation is going.

"That's what you were *told*, but that doesn't mean that's what's *true*." When Turn scoffs, Mark leans in closer and looks him right in the eyes. "You aren't even *born* yet, Turn. You won't be until 1982."

"Whoa," Bobbie says in a long and drawn-out way, "that's heavy."

"Heavy *bull*-shit," Turn says, chuckling and smiling and looking at the others. A few smile as well, but many others do not.

"I can prove it to you, Turn…if you want me to," Mark says to him. He reaches into his jacket pocket and pulls out a small black object that looks like a pen, just without the pointed end where you write.

"What's that?" Turn says, his eyes narrowing.

"It's a flash stick, something we usually use to *take* memories, but in cases where it's been used on an individual before, we can *return* those memories."

"I don't need no damn flash stick!" Turn says, his earlier smile now turning to a sneer of anger.

"Really?" Mark says. "Then tell me…when *were* you born?"

Turn chuckles. "That's easy, my birthday is…" He trails-off as he realized he can't seem to remember. "It's…" He bites his lip and glances around at the others nervously. "I…I don't *know*."

Mark holds up the flash stick before Turn's face. "Would you like to?"

Turn bites his lip even harder, then gives a slight nod. Mark nods as well, then moves the flash stick closer to Turn's face, to his ear and then behind it. He pushes the button and there's a slight flash. Mark pulls his arm away and looks at Turn, who's blinking rapidly, as if coming out of a deep sleep.

"Soldier," Mark says, looking into Turn's eyes, "when were you born?"

"December 12, 1982," Turn says. No hesitation.

"Regimental history."

Turn straightens-up, as if giving a report to a superior…which in a way he is. "I Marine Expeditionary Force, joined-up September 12, 2001, the day after the towers fell. Finished basic November 21. Shipped out to Afghanistan on December 4, saw action at Tora Bora, Zormat, and of course Kabul. Tour ended December 2002. Rejoined, went back to Afghanistan for a few months, then shipped to Iraq. Invaded Baghdad in April 2003. Last mission was in Fallujah on…"

"On December 22," Mark finishes for him, "the day you lost your legs…the day that started you on leaving *your* time to enter this one."

"*Damn!*" Bobbie says, while beside him Walter whistles.

"It's a lot to take in, I know," Mark says, "I've experienced it before myself."

"What about me?" Bobbie asks. "Have *I* experienced it?"

Mark takes in a deep breath and looks off before answering. "Although I haven't seen your file…well, the fact that you're a super soldier makes it likely."

Bobbie nods at the flash stick still in Mark's hand. "Can…can you?"

Mark nods again and just as he did with Turn, he leans forward and puts the flash stick up against the back of Bobbie's ear. It flashes, and a moment later Bobbie is sitting back with that same dazed and confused look that Turn just had.

"*Well?*" Walter says.

"I joined up in 2018…on my 18th birthday." He chuckles a mirthless chuckle. "Just in time for World War Three."

"That was a helluva conflict," Mark says, "one that was instrumental in getting the 177th off the ground in the first place."

"The 177th?" Turn says.

"The 177th Time Travel Division based out of Area 51," Mark replies. "Its heyday was, or *will be*, the years 2030 to 2036." He smiles. "That's when John Titor was in command."

Blank stares from Turn and Bobbie meet those words, and Mark can't help but chuckle to himself. *Did I look the same way the first time I heard it?* He figures he did.

"Look," he says, growing serious once more, "we've got some time to kill. Let me explain."

29 – THE 177TH

"It started with Project Pegasus, which was a classified, defense-related research and development program headed up by the Defense Advanced Research Projects Agency…or DARPA," Mark begins. "The science behind it was based on the work Nikola Tesla did in 1943 when he developed schematics for a teleportation machine based on radiant energy. This type of energy had the power to bend space-time and would form a shimmering curtain between two elliptical booms. Going into that curtain would put you into a vortal tunnel that would instantly deliver you to your desired time and space."

"God," Turn says.

Mark nods. "It gets worse. They used children, as the strains of moving between the past, present and future was easier to handle at that age. Still, as the program really got going in the 60s, problems cropped-up. For instance, one poor young boy came back from his temporal voyage before his legs. He was writing in pain on the floor, stumps where his legs had been."

"Jesus," Bennewitz says this time, "I never heard that one."

"Happened in '71…was awful," Walter says, shaking his head as if remembering it firsthand. *Maybe he does*, Turn thinks.

"Anyways, Mark continues, "John Titor is the man who knows the most when it comes to time travel."

Turn rolls his eyes. "Well, if I never heard of Project Pegasus or all the rest of it, you know I've never heard of…"

"Commander John Titor," Mark says. "First joined up with

Florida's Fighting Diamondbacks when he was just 13-years-old, though on an alternate timeline from ours, and in the year 2011. That lasted until 2015 when WWIII started, though the conflict was just a continuation of the Second American Civil War which had started in 2008."

"Still followin'?" Bennewitz says, looking over at Turn with a big grin on his face.

"Man, I stopped followin' back when Paul introduced himself," Turn says with a chuckle, "now all I do is listen and hope some of it sticks."

"Good enough," Mark says, and goes on. "The US split into five separate regions and the fighting went on for years. During that time Titor stuck with the US government – now located in Omaha, Nebraska – and joined their Air Force, becoming an officer and pilot."

"And can you guess where he was stationed at?" Bennewitz asks, a hint of a smile turning up one corner of his mouth as he looks at Turn.

"No, but I bet you're gonna tell me."

"Dulce."

"*Shit.*"

Bennewitz smiles and nods. "He was one of the first to fly the TR-3B spacecraft…or what we might think of as those triangular-shaped UFOs."

"His real test came in 2036, however," Mark says, taking up the story. "By that time – and in that particular *timeframe* – time travel had been perfected to such an extent that a whole wing of the Air Force was dedicated to it."

"This was the 177th Time Travel Division," Bennewitz says. "Titor commanded it, and that all came about because of one mission he was on, the most critical mission the world has seen."

"It all goes back to 1975, the year that IBM created their 5100 computer, a model that ran on APL and BASIC programming…two languages that relied on a signed 32-bit integer storage system."

"Tell it to me in English," Turn says.

"The 5100 could only calculate time and dates from 1975 until January 19, 2038. After that they'd suffer an internal meltdown, effectively bringing down their computer-reliant society with them."

"If that happened it'd be back to cave man days," Mark says, "and that's why Titor was chosen to go back to 1975 to get an original IBM 5100 so as to debug those still propping up the systems in 2038."

"Titor was chosen because his grandpa had helped build the damn things back in the day, if you can believe that!" Bennewitz says with a laugh.

Shit, I'll believe anything *at this point*, Turn thinks to himself, but just nods silently.

"Anyways," Mark says, "we should get back to the problem at hand. What we have to focus on now is the Trifecta, or dad's original plan to take this planet back."

"And where in God's Name do we start?" Walter says.

Mark smirks. "Why, the time shed…where else?"

30 – THE TIME SHED

The Gates of the Mountains north of Helena, Montana
Friday, May 25, 1979
4:30 PM

The six men move down the smooth tunnel-like-hallways of the old Montana base, making their way to the room that holds the time shed. They hurry down one of hallway after another, turning corners here, passing doors there, and sometimes moving down stairs. Turn has no idea when it'll end. Finally they turn a corner, see a door, and move through it. It's another set of stairs and the men take them quickly, sometimes two at a time as they head down into the lower levels of the base.

"Listen, if we want to make this work we've got to get back into Dulce and we've got to do it around the time of the attack," Bennewitz says as they move down the stairs.

Stu narrows his eyes and gives Bennewitz a sideways look. "Why Dulce and why at the time of attack?"

"Dulce because that's the only place we're going to find a time shed, and around the attack because that's the only time the Grays and the Reptilians will be distracted enough for them to let their guard down around that area."

"Blue Lake's got a shed," Walter says.

"Too dangerous now," Mark replies.

"*Time shed?*" Turn says. It's not the first time he's asked, but he hopes this time he won't be ignored.

Bennewitz rolls his eyes to that, but Walter is able to answer Turn's question before the wild-eyed man gets a word in.

"A time shed is a small room that acts as a time machine – simply walk inside, close the door, and let the room do all the work." He cocks his head to one side. "It's really quite simple, and the Grays have the right idea. You see, to do time travel you always need lots of quartz crystals. They burn up quickly, meaning if you want to do a lot of jumps, you'll need a lot of crystals."

"And they're hard to come by," Mark adds. "Here on Earth we're blessed to have quite a lot under the ground, and close to the surface. Hell, even rock hounds dig 'em out…and year round!"

"Other planets aren't so fortunate, including the Gray's home world of Zeta Reticuli."

"And the Reptilians' home world of Draco," Bennewitz adds, looking impatient that this even needs to be explained at all. To his way of thinking, *everyone* should know what a time shed is.

"Besides being hard to come by, they burn up damn fast if you're not using them properly," Walter continues, and just as the men reach the bottom of the stairs and come out into yet another hallway. "That's always been one of the major problems with our time sheds at places like Blue Lake and Kirtland Air Force Base. The time shed in Dulce, however…well…"

"Well what?" Bobbie says.

"Well, the Grays built it damn good so you can typically get three jumps to a crystal, unlike the time shed in say Blue Lake, which might give you one."

"*If* you're lucky," Mark adds, and Walter nods to that.

"And by going back into Dulce we *will* be lucky," Bennewitz says. "While the Grays and the Reptilians are focused on the attacks at the entrance and those down below, we'll use the time shed here to zap into Dulce, get to Level 3 where that time shed is, and from there we can branch out with our three-prong plan."

"Alright, that's it…I'm leavin'," Turn says, shaking his head as he stops walking and makes to turn around. The others look at him with narrowed eyes, unsure of what has set him off.

"Turn, what–"

"Time sheds….crystals…Black Knight…this damn soul catcher – hell, I don't know shit!" Turn casts an accusatory look the others' way. "Why the hell am I here anyways? I don't know *half* of what you guys seem to know." Mark tries to get a word in but Turn puts his hand up, staying him while he continues to speak. "And now this three-prong plan? *Shit* – when does it end?"

"It ends soon, Turn, it ends damn soon." Mark moves over and claps him on the shoulder as he says the words, and Turn gives a slight nod. He might be perturbed and feeling more lost than ever, but at least he knows he's around friends.

"And it's not like you haven't used the Dulce time shed before," Walter says, looking from the others to Turn. "That's how Anderholt brings you men over, the men from other times…whether 30 years in the future like you, Turn, or 30 years in the past sometimes."

"Though we don't take too many men from the ol' World War Two days anymore," Mark says, shaking his head. "Too polite."

Turn narrows his eyes to that, not sure what Mark is getting at, but a moment later the pilot and off-worlder breaks out into a smile, then starts chuckling. The others soon join in, a nice ice-breaker exactly when one was needed. They quiet down after that, letting their thoughts take over as they continue down the hallway. After another minute they're there, at a door marked simply with the words, 'storage room.'

"Well, this is it," Bennewitz says, looking at everyone but especially Turn and Bobbie, for which everything is new.

He opens the door.

31 – THE TRIFECTA

The time shed room was an old room. Antiquated was a better word, for the room had a terribly inefficient crystal burning mechanism. It'd have to work, however, for their plan depended upon getting back into Dulce. Besides flying the pilfered UFO they got on the mothership, using the time shed to get in was their only other option.

"There's always the front door," Bennewitz had said when the topic had been discussed shortly before, but that just got him a lot of cold looks and eye rolls.

The way the Trifecta plan was set forth, the men would split into three teams.

"Stu will get back into Blue Lake just after the attack on Dulce and right as the debriefing's getting underway–"

"And more importantly," Bennewitz had cut in on Mark there when the plan was first explained, just before they began walking down those tunnels, "as the dead are carted back in."

"The *dead?*" Turn had said.

Mark had nodded. "That's how we'll go after their soul catcher. Stu will lead that team, and Donlon will be on it…once Stu informs him of that fact."

Mark had looked up and Stu had nodded his understanding so Mark continued.

"The second team – with Bobbie in the lead – will go back to Blue Lake in the here and now, picking up those men that know of our plans and are eager to help."

"And they are?" Turn had asked.

"Well, so far we know that we've still got Chargin' Charlie, Emil, John, Fred, David and Moses at the base and on our side…though not all of them know it."

"Many are just like you, Turn – from another time and not in on all the details of what's going on, what the *true* story is."

"But we'll tell 'em," Bennewitz had said, a crazy smile coming across his face. "And when we do, we'll be ready for the second prong of our plan…Russia."

"*Russia?*" Turn had said. "What the hell's in Russia?"

"An old, crashed UFO that came down in '91," Mark had said before scoffing, "*1991*, that is."

"So it hasn't even happened yet," Turn had said.

"Well, not in *this* time," Mark had answered, "though from your own time period, it's been there for 12 years."

"And inside her we'll gain the answer to an important secret," Bennewitz had said.

The third and final team would also be heading back to Blue Lake, getting there just as the Dutchman was about to be killed. The hope was to figure out who the traitors in their midst were.

"I'd like to be leading that team," Mark had said, then sighed, "but I'm the most trained for the moon so that's what it'll be."

"We'll find the bastards that are responsible for your father, don't worry," Walter had said, and no one had argued with that. Still, if anyone was going to find out who had killed the Dutchman, it'd most likely be his son. That'd be awfully hard to do when he was 239,000 miles away, though.

The six men continued down those smooth tunnels and finally came to the place they'd been seeking – the base's time shed.

"There it is," Mark says, pointing at the nondescript door on the otherwise nondescript tunnel wall. It said "storage room" and that was it.

"It'll go faster if we're not all inside, blocking the magnetic resonances," Stu says as they stop in front of it.

"You're up first," Bennewitz says, a bit of impatience in his voice. "Then it's you, Bobbie."

"You ready?" Walter asks, looking to Stu.

Stu lets out a whistle. "Hope so, but I gotta say…it'll sure be weird heading back to Blue Lake just shortly after the mission debriefing." He chuckles. "I hope my better half is up to it."

"He better be," Mark says. "You know the Soul Catcher is the first stage of the plan, and which everything else depends on."

"I'm up to it," Stu says as he looks down at the floor. He takes in a deep breath before letting it out slowly, then looks back at Mark. "I just hope Tommy is."

"He was trained for it," Walter says, "and he knew what he signed-up for."

"Yeah, but in the training he was never…"

"*Dead?*" Bobbie says, then looks to the others. "Because Tommy *is* dead, ya'll know that, right?"

"Hell, Bobbie," Turn says with a laugh, "if time isn't a boundary for these guys then I don't think death will be either."

Mark chuckles at that and claps Turn on the shoulder. "If you only knew the half of it."

"What, is there another one of those flash sticks I missed out on?"

Everyone has a good laugh to that, and then when things quiet down the attention goes back to Stu.

"Well, this is it," he says. "We've trained for this for some time."

"And we're ready," Mark says, then, "And one more thing, Stu…remember to tell someone *what time* Aaron gets back from that Gray mothership he fled to."

Stu nods. "Will do. Now…good luck, everyone."

"Good luck, Stu," they all say, and with that the astronaut opens the door and heads inside.

PART VI

32 – PAST AND FUTURE

Blue Lake
Friday, May 25, 1979
4:32 AM

Colonel Stu Roosevelt, the commander of the Material Acquisitions Team that'd destroyed Dulce Base with his CED device – or at least everything living inside of the base – walks down one of the Blue Lake hallways. The post-mission debriefing that Ellis just gave is on his mind, though not as much as getting some sleep is. He rounds another corner and there's his room's hallway. He moves past a few doors until he gets to one marked "107," takes out his keys, unlocks it, and steps inside. He swipes his hand against the wall where the light switch is, illuminating the small quarters. He's so caught-up in his thoughts that he doesn't notice that the rocking chair next to the bed is occupied. As he moves to the desk on the other side of the room, however, he's made aware of it.

"Ahem," comes a clearing of the throat.

Stu stops dead in his tracks and for the first time looks up and over. There, sitting in the old wooden rocking chair, is…himself.

"Stu, I've got to tell you something and I've got to tell it to you fast," the man that looks just like him says to Stu.

"What…who…" Stu manages, but the man looking just like him puts his hand up and starts talking once again.

"We've started Trifecta."

That sobers Stu up right away, and all thoughts of who this man is or what he's doing here go from his mind. His years of training take over.

"When?"

"A few hours from now, though with the way the time sheds work it's a little tricky to keep track."

"Right," Stu says, knowing exactly what his counterpart – who he now knows is his future self – is talking about. "When do I start?"

"You don't. I do."

"*What?* That was never part of the plan! How are we–"

"Plans change. You'll find that out real quick in another…" the counterpart glances down at his watch, "…two and a half hours." He looks back up at Stu. "Now, what I need *you* to do is carry on as normal, go about your business, and then when the shit hits the fan – and you'll know when it does – you hightail it to the nearest safe spot and hold up. Then, come 1538 hours, you get your ass to the basement and the teleporter there. You're going to Montana."

Stu takes it all in and then a few moments after his counterpart stops talking he sits down on the bed. After a couple more moments he looks up.

"How bad is it?" he asks.

"It's bad, but not unwinnable."

Stu shrugs. "Then I guess I'll do my best."

The future Stu rises up and claps his past self on the shoulder. "I know you will, and remember…I'm counting on you."

Stu scoffs to that. *Hell, I wrote the book on the physics of time travel…I should know!* He says nothing, however, and a few moments later his future self is up and heading out the door. Stu watches him go, and gives a silent prayer for his safety.

33 – SOUL CATCHER

Blue Lake
Friday, May 25, 1979
4:41 AM

Corporal Tommy Wynn's body hits the cold steel slab.

"Damn it," Donlon nearly shouts, "take it easy, will ya!"

"Relax," Stu says, looking as calm and cool and collected as ever. He'd been happy with how the conversation with his past self went, and he'd found Donlon shortly thereafter, explaining it all to him. After that they'd caught-up with the guards escorting the Dulce Base dead. Major Fred Sayer had been with them, and knowing he could trust the young soldier, Stu allowed him to tag along to the secluded hospital wing of the base. They'd need all the help they could get in this time, he knew.

"What do you mean, 'relax,' doc?" Donlon says as he put his hands on his hips and sticks out his chest. The military brass on his lapel glares out at Stu. "We just got wiped out back there and Tommy here's dead – how the hell do you expect me to *relax*?"

"He's not dead," Stu says.

"Not…not…*not dead?*" Fred says. "What the hell do ya mean, he's not dead! He's got a Goddamn piece of vat glass the size of my fist stickin' out the side of his head, for Chrissakes!"

Stu ignores Fred's words, not even looking up at the soldier or the stone-jawed colonel, who stands there gritting his teeth and seething. Instead the astronaut walks up to the young Vietnam vet's body and puts his fingers near the throat, the temples, and then the eyes. He kneels down and listens at the heart, prods the stomach. Finally he looks back at Donlon. "We've got about thirty seconds to flat line him the way we want."

"Flat line him, doc? We're supposed to be *saving* him, not *killing* him!"

"Tommy knew what he was signing up for, Colonel," Stu says calmly, though his body was anything but. He's moving about quickly now, gathering up the needed materials and supplies. He only has one shot at this, he knows, and quite literally.

"What are you talkin' about, doc?"

Stu finally looks up at Fred, the major standing there with his arms crossed trying to look as mean and authoritative as he could, though the confusion was beginning to creep into his eyes. He fidgets and shifts nervously – Stu was up to something, and he didn't like it.

"Back in '68 we started a program called "Etheria," Stu says as he starts attaching a few diodes and clasps to Tommy's body. "It was designed to get us as close to the Grays as we possibly could – right up to their soul catchers."

"Soul catchers…" Fred says, trailing off. An underground alien base was one thing, but now it seemed even this was going a bit far.

"A bit much, isn't it?" Donlon says, and Fred can only nod.

Stu affixes a final clasp to one of Tommy's fingers and then looks back at Fred. "We've got to stop them, Fred, we've got to stop them stealing our souls."

And with that he hits the button on the bedside machine, sending 700 volts of electricity through the Tommy's body. A few moments later the defibrillator machine's line goes flat.

~~~

Light suddenly bursts into Tommy's vision, though it's yellow and bright and white and everything that the sun or overhead lighting is not. Then he realizes that he's on the ceiling, or at least in the upper corner of the room. Most strange of all, however, was the sight of his own body on the cold steel slab of the makeshift operating room. It's then that Tommy knows he'ss dead. It's not until a few moments later, however, when Stu turns around and begins looking up at the ceiling, waving his hand as he does so, that Tommy knows Etheria
~~~

had been activated.

My God, he thinks as he floats there, disembodied and lifeless*, I really* am *dead…we really are doing this….we–*

"Tommy."

Tommy's thoughts are cutoff as Stu calls out his name, still looking toward the ceiling. The young soldier knows that Stu knows he's there.

"Tommy, I know you're here," Stu says next. "We're going with Etheria, we're going to try and buck the light. You were killed in Dulce but the shot we gave you years ago was waiting to kick in, and it did. It kept your brain functions alive and attached to your body. Now you're on your own." Stu reaches over and grabs hold of some kind of medical devices that his hands wrap around, then holds them up. "You've got twenty minutes, Tommy, twenty minutes before I jerk you back to life…*if* I can." He looks down, a tinge of sadness coming to his face, but only for a moment before he looks up again. "We'll get you back, Tommy, don't you worry about that, we'll get you back, just don't go toward the light, whatever you do, don't–"

Stu's words are cutoff, though only to Tommy. For it's at that instant that a bright white tunnel of light suddenly appears before him, blocking out all other sights and sounds. It's warm, inviting, and contains all the love in the world. Tommy wants to go to it, desperately wants to go to it, but he holds himself back. It's a trick, he knows, for his Etheria training has taught him such.

A moment later the white light seems to sense this, sense his apprehension, for it pulsates, sends out more warm feelings, but in the midst of that, Tommy notices the slightest trace of coldness, fear, and hate. The light notices that he notices, and that's when the room around him drops away, and he's suddenly in the deep blackness of space.

Fear grips Tommy, though a kind he'd never known before. This is the fear that can only come to the dead, when they know that death won't even save them from the unspeakable horror that suddenly confronts them. Tommy is confronted with that now, and he doesn't know if he can take it.

The training back at Blue Lake in '68 had been explicit – the light would only last for the length of a meal.

They'd all questioned that, but that's all the instructor could tell them. It wasn't an exact science, after all, dying and seeing a light and then not going toward it.

To most it'd flown in the face of every notion they'd ever had. You should *always* go toward the light, for that light held your family, friends, and eventually God. It was all a trick, though, one designed by the Grays to steal the souls before they could pass to that place that the white light was thought to signify. The Grays needed the souls, for they had none. Something about the soul's energy fed them, though not like food fed a dying man; more like how a drug fed a junkie's fix.

No one knew how long it'd been going on, the harvesting of souls, but the American government had known about it since the year after Eisenhower signed the treaty. That's when they began exploring it, researching it, trying to figure out how it worked.

It took ten years, but they'd done it, though the cost had been high. More than three dozen men had volunteered to be killed on a table, their heart stopped with anesthetic or electric shocks. All were promised that they'd be brought back. None of them had been, not a one.

Tommy knew that, knew it right away when Stu called out to him in that hospital room. He was thirty-one, and there'd be no coming back.

He firms his resolve. He's a soldier, one meant to fight Grays. If they wanted a fight, he'd give 'em one. The light pulses, sensing his decision, knowing it has another.

Tommy feels the pulse, senses the love, but also the underlying 'something' that isn't quite right lying right under the surface. He backs off, fled, overcoming his fear and goes out into the deep blackness of space. He's going still when the feeling of aloneness hits him for the first time. He looks back, and the light is gone.

All around him is blackness, the blackness of space, the void, nothingness…death.

And then something else happens. It isn't a light, but more a *feeling*. The overpowering feeling of love and life and friends and happiness. Tommy knows this is the true light, the one that most miss, the one the Grays can only block for a short time.

Tommy goes toward it, goes toward it and hopes he's right. The fate of Man's soul is riding on it.

34 – FIRE ON THE MOON

Earth Orbit
Friday, May 25, 1979
6:38 PM

After seeing Stu and Bobbie off – the former to earlier that morning to take care of the soul catcher, the latter to a time in the afternoon to get Charlie and the Blue Lake team together – it was Walter and Bennewitz's turn. They take the teleporter to Blue Lake, arriving at their current time. Walter heads off to find to find Eddie and Stan and convince them to commandeer a craft and take it to Russia in the near future, while Bennewitz goes to find Heather.

For his part, Mark stays back at the base in Montana with Turn, going to the deeper levels to find the ship he's looking for. It's a standard Pleiadian vessel, typically called a "Nordic disc," both because the Pleiadians were also known as the Nordic race of aliens and because the ship looked like the classic 'flying saucer' of the 1950s, although much more futuristic as well. It looks to be one solid chunk of chromium steel, though Mark knows it's actually hundreds if not thousands of parts welded together with advanced technology that humans can only dream of. The Nordic disc stretches over 100 feet across though comes in at just 20 feet wide. Mark also knows that those dimensions aren't quite accurate, and that when he gets into the craft it'll seem no bigger than a living room, and also that it could morph and shift and even skip dimensions. There'd be no need for the latter – Mark hopes – but he will need to get the appropriate landing bay doors of the Montana base open if he wants to get the disc airborne. A short time later he and Turn have done so, and just in time to see both Bennewitz and Heather come back via the teleporter. At that point the four of them are ready to go.

That'd been nearly an hour ago, and now the three of them are racing out of Earth's orbit, the moon in the Nordic disc's large front window and getting closer by the second. As they travel thousands of miles per hour, their conversation drifts to the motherships they'll soon encounter, as well as those scattered around the solar system.

"I'm telling you," Bennewitz was saying, "it's not just *a* base, but dozens of 'em, all underground."

Mark cocks his head to one side at the words. "Yeah, that theory'd hold water too…if it wasn't for what those monks saw back in the 12th Century."

"That was a *long* time ago," Heather says with an eye roll, "things change."

"*Twelfth Century?*" Turn says. He looks from Mark to Heather to Bennewitz and back again. Finally Mark sighs and begins to speak.

"Back on June 18th, in the year 1178, a group of five monks at an abbey in Canterbury reported seeing flames shooting out from the backside of the moon, reporting later that the upper horn of the moon split in two."

"My God," Heather says, "I haven't heard this one before."

Mark nods. "Most haven't. Reports tell us that the monks saw a flaming torch spring up and then spew out fire and hot coals and sparks over a *considerable* distance. They said the moon was throbbing like a wounded snake before returning to normal…though just for a short time. The monks saw dozens of fiery shows like the first that night, and when it was all said and done the moon had taken on a blackish appearance."

"Today we call the area the Giordano Bruno crater," Bennewitz says, taking up the tale. "When the area was studied three years ago it was determined that it's 22 kilometers in width and that when it was created it kicked up 10 million tons of debris."

"That much debris would have created a week-long, blizzard-like meteor storm here on Earth, however," Mark says, shaking his head. "Nothing like that is recorded as happening anywhere on the Earth back in 1178."

"That's why it's figured that crater was actually formed about three hundred and fifty *million* years ago, not eight hundred," Bennewitz says.

"And what's the *real* truth?" Turn asks.

Mark and Bennewitz look at one another before answering, as if they want to get their stories straight and some unspoken eye communication would ensure that'd happen. Mark nods to Turn's question.

"The real truth is that we haven't been alone on this planet, *ever*. Worse, we're being controlled and manipulated and the leaders of our government aren't working for us, but for the aliens. It's always been this way, for hundreds of years.

"Hundreds of years?" Turn says. "Oh, *please!*"

"Believe it or not," Mark says, "but it's the truth. The main problem were the Grays and their time-traveling motherships," Bennewitz says. "In 1645, it was reported that 'a large moon' was seen near Venus, and was seen coming and going until 1767. The same craft were seen near Venus in 1787, 1788 and 1789…and if you think they didn't play a role in starting the French Revolution, think again."

"Yeah, but what does this all have to do with us now, and with this base you say exists on the moon?" Turn asks.

"Keep listening, it'll come…I hope," Heather says with a smile.

"Yeah, about the moon," Mark says from the front of the ship. "In 1783 and 1787, huge bright lights were reported on the moon. Mistakenly reported as volcanoes, they then lit up the dark side of the moon. This was the start of the Gray's base there, or more aptly, the Reptilian off-world presence through the Grays."

"And they keep comin'," Bennewitz says. "In February 1894, a comet was photographed striking a large dark object in our solar system. It happened to have wings, and according to the Andromedans, this was a Draconian mothership. The same type of incidents happened in the vicinity of Mars on November 25, 1894, when a large ship was seen illuminating part of Mars. It was the same thing that'd happened with Mercury in 1789 and then the Sun in 1859. This same body sits out there today and has been dubbed Vulcan. In reality it's a large mothership."

"But we're not alone, and not without friends," Mark says. "During the total eclipse of July 29, 1878, astronomers saw two large planetary bodies the size of Venus between Mercury and Venus.

According to the Andromedans, these bodies were Pleiadian and Andromedan motherships that had traveled back in time and were observing the Grays, who were at the time orbiting around the Sun."

"And that was a hundred years ago," Bennewitz says. "They've been coming more and more since then. The same phenomena occurred on April 4, 1892, and that Draconian ship was about one third the size of the moon, about 700 miles in diameter, and it had wings. Another Draconian mothership was observed on January 27, 1912. It was 250 miles in length and 50 miles wide and resembled a crow. It was sitting on the moon, docking at the base and…well, what the hell are they doin' there, Mark?"

"God only knows," Mark says, shaking his head, "and all we can do is pity the poor souls that wound up there, souls that we sent."

"Whoa…wait a minute!" Heather says. "You're telling me there are *people* on those motherships?"

Bennewitz nods. "It all gets back to the May 1954 treaty that Ike signed with the Grays at Holloman Air Force Base." He scoffs. "That treaty screwed us *a lot* more than we ever could have known."

Mark speaks up too. "Pretty much tied the hands of the Andromedan Council. After that there was nothing the benevolent alien races could do to take a more active role in our evolution. In effect, it's placed the burden squarely on the shoulders of humanity to enlighten itself. It'd be our task to create ascension on an individual basis. From that point on, outside help has been unavailable to us."

"What's worse is how badly we fell for it, for what the Grays were selling," Bennewitz says. "At the time of the Holloman agreement we had an exchange of military personnel with the Grays, giving over 16 of our men so they could travel to the Gray's home world." He shakes his head and makes a fist, and Turn can see his face quivering in anger. "It was all a lie, though. According to what that Andromedans told us later, it was really *109* humans that were taken…and not to Zeta Reticuli where the Grays are from, but to some of the motherships they've got parked behind our solar system's planets!"

Mark nods. "Some even got taken to the alien bases on Mar's second moon, Phobos."

"What happened to them?" Turn asks after Mark pauses.

"They were experimented on," Mark says, "the same as all those we found down in Dulce."

"They were the first," Bennewitz says, "and after that taste, the Grays couldn't get enough." He looks up at Mark. "What'd your dad say over the radio…*30,000* captives were down in Dulce when we attacked it? My God!"

"So this isn't just a search and destroy mission," Turn says, "it's a rescue mission too."

"If it can turn into that, so much the better," Mark says.

"Whoa, rescue mission?" Heather says. "How are we gonna rescue 109 people – if that many are even still alive – in this dinky little ship?"

Mark laughs. "Remember how I said I could fly anything, even a bathtub with wings?" There are some groans from the back to that. "Well, the same holds true for these Gray motherships."

"Oh, you've *got* to be kidding!" Heather says. "A *mothership?*"

"Where the hell would you even *land* something that size," Turn says. "What is it, about the size of a football field?"

"More like the size of New Hampshire."

"*New Hampshire!*" Heather says.

"Oh, c'mon, Mark…it's not that big," Bennewitz says, shrugging. "Rhode Island, *maybe*."

"Where the hell you gonna land a spaceship the size of a state?" Turn says, his eyes wide and incredulous.

"Yeah, the White House lawn won't exactly do, Mark," Bennewitz says. "What exactly did you have in mind?"

Mark glances back to look at Bennewitz. "You've been keeping up on the news in 1979…where are those SALT II talks happening?"

"Vienna, but…Mark, no…no, Mark, just no."

Mark smiles as he looks back at the controls and the wide window looking out into space, but says nothing. There, far off in the distance, is the moon. The dark side is waiting for them, and Mark considers punching the ship to take them there all the faster. Instead he looks to his left, out the window and then back down at the radar.

The Black Knight satellite is there. Without telling anyone, Mark slowly begins to steer them toward it.

35 – BACK IN THE USSR

400 miles east of Tien Shan Mountains, Kyrgyzstan
Thursday, August 28, 1991
4:47 PM

After leaving the Montana base, Walter had tracked-down both Stan and Eddie. It wasn't hard to do – both of the MAT Team astronauts were in their usual lab, going over some of the hardware they'd recovered from Dulce. What *was* hard to do was convincing the two of them that he wasn't dead. Mentioning Trifecta finally did it, and after that they were all ears. All told it took 17 minutes for Walter to track them down, convince them of what was going on, and then have the two of them commandeer the same ship that Eddie had flown out of Dulce the night before. After that they were off.

Eddie simply called the craft they were in "the triangle." The thing looked like a triangle with a small, glass-enclosed cockpit area nestled down into its body, although it wasn't glass, but something else. Eddie wasn't real clear on that, only that he'd seen the same at Los Alamos and knew the secret military teams were working on creating something similar using the same alien technology. They weren't quite there yet, but that didn't preclude test flying the one they'd captured. Eddie had been such a pilot, and that's why flying the thing from Dulce had been so easy.

The triangle was now racing over the snowy mountains of northern China and southern Russia. Eddie wasn't sure which country they belonged to, and he didn't much care. There was no way either a Russian MiG-29 travelling at its top speed of 1,367 miles per hour, or a Chinese Xian JH-7 travelling at its top speed of 1,092 miles per hour was going to catch him. Currently he was cruising at 4,600 miles per hour, or Mach 6. Eddie was still surprised at how well the craft handled at that speed, and he wondered what kinds of speeds the Grays usually got these machines up to. Of course, he knew, it could be a Reptilian craft as well. Either way, Eddie had been having one helluva good time trying the craft out. Nothing could compare to that initial flight out of Dulce Base, however, when Eddie had taken the craft off the landing port's floor. Now here he was, 7,200 miles from Dulce and 12 years as well. *Time travel*, he thought with a chuckle, and took a moment to glance over his shoulder.

Behind him in the UFO were Walter and Stan. It'd been Walter that'd come into their Blue Lake hangar a few hours earlier to tell them that Trifecta had started up. Walter hadn't needed to say anymore – both Stan and Eddie had known about the plan for years, ever since the first attempts to take Dulce back had started. So after getting over their initial shock they'd listened to Walter, nodded a lot, and then got down to business. Now here they were, racing to a UFO crash site…one that wasn't set to see a UFO crash there for another 13 minutes.

Stan glances down at his watch. "It's coming up soon, about ten minutes now."

"I can't believe we know of a crash *before* it happens," Walter says.

"There's a lot we know," Eddie says from his spot at the controls, "and a lot the public doesn't…even people like you, Walter, people on the inside but not totally in-the-know."

"*So…*" Walter says, narrowing his eyes and taking on a conspiratorial look, "how'd this all get started? I've heard a lot, but I haven't heard this one. We've got ten minutes – fill me in."

Eddie looks to Stan, back at Walter, and then down to the floor.

"That tale's not for everyone," Stan says.

"Well, I'm not everyone," Walter replies.

"Alright," Eddie says, looking back up from the floor, "if you want to hear it, then here it goes." He pauses, looks off for a moment as if trying to find the best place to begin, and then launches into it.

"It started in Russia, in 1991…though maybe *ahead* would be a better term to use."

"Just tell the story," Stan says, rolling his eyes.

"Alright, it starts in Russia. Just around the time people are startin' to get off work for the day an extremely large object suddenly appears over the Caspian Sea. It measures 600 meters in length and another 110 in diameter. Radar shows it moving at a fast clip, 6,300 miles per hour."

Walter whistles, and Eddie nods.

"At that point it was at 21,000 feet. An alert goes out and two MIG 29 fighters start heading for the Mangyshlak Peninsula where this thing's been spotted. The two pilots are ordered to force the craft down" – Eddie scoffs here – "can you imagine two 52x35-foot planes tryin' to force down somethin' that's nearly 2,000 feet long and another 360 feet across?" He chuckles. "Anyways, they try that over the Aral Sea and – surprise, surprise – *that* doesn't work so the order comes through for them to *shoot* the thing down." He laughs outright now. "First the two fighters close from 2,600 feet to 1,600, the better to fire a couple warning shots across the thing's flight path. Well, when they get set to fire, guess what? No response from their controls. On top of it their electrical systems stop working. *Everything* in their cockpits are suddenly dead! With engines sputtering, the order is given for the fighters to nurse their way home, which they manage to do."

"And the UFO?" Walter says. "That's what it was…wasn't it?"

Eddie nods. "About forty-five minutes after they broke off their engagement with the thing it vanishes from radar. That actually sent a wave of relief through the military men that were tracking the thing, for it was clear this was something beyond their capabilities to understand. That sense of relief didn't last for long, however. It took a bit of time, but a day or two later word began to filter out of the small villages around Karakol that an immense object had crashed. A private expedition was organized to go in and check it out. For two weeks they trekked up to the area, a desolate and isolated spot in the mountains of Shaitan Mazar."

"And into a rocky gorge called 'The Grave of the Devil,'" Stan adds.

"That was the place," Eddie continues with a nod. "Several of the locals had already gone up to the crash site, and several of them claimed that they'd been burned while many more claimed that their watches had stopped working once in the area. Finally in November, nearly three months after the initial encounter between the craft and the two fighters, the expedition reached the site. They discovered what the government had kept from the public, and not just the crash. You see, shortly after the crash a helicopter had been ordered in to help hoist part of the object off of the snow-covered bank of the gorge. Something went wrong and the helicopter crashed, killing everyone on board. After that the Russian government gave up."

"Did they go back?" Walter asks.

"Not until spring when the weather was better," Eddie answers, "…but they hadn't been counting on this private expedition to get up there first. That private expedition likely experienced what the military had – the defenses the object had to protect itself. The members of the expedition began to feel an overwhelming amount of energy in the air, and that while they were still fifteen hundred meters from the craft. They pressed on, but when they were a thousand meters from it that overwhelming amount of energy changed to an intense feeling of dread and anxiety. They pressed on nonetheless, but only made it a few more feet before an overwhelming feeling of fatigue overtook them. They could go no farther, and didn't. Satisfying themselves with a few drawings of the object, they left."

"And did they or anyone else ever go back?" Walter asks.

Stan shakes his head. "Russian military got back in there and sealed the place off. Today – or at least what *will be* today – there's nothing left."

"Russians got it?"

"Maybe…maybe not."

"What do you mean?"

"Well, that level of fear and dread the expedition members were feeling. Those reactions were never recorded in 1989 when another UFO went down in Russia, this time one that the military managed to retrieve…and with a still-living alien."

"*Whoa!*" Walter says. "I can't believe I've never heard this!"

"Hardly anyone has," Stan says.

At the controls, Eddie chuckles to himself. "You're about to…*oh boy*, you're about to!"

36 – PLAYING BOTH SIDES

Blue Lake
Friday, May 25, 1979
4:47 AM

General Anderholt continues to lean against the wall of the hangar, watching as the men file out. The mission debriefing that Ellis has just given is ending, the men going to get some chow and then some much-needed sleep. Well, that wouldn't be true for all of them, the general knows, just the soldiers from the CAT teams. The MAT Team members would be going to their labs or their hangars, working on all the new technology they'd seized or questioning all the prisoners that'd been freed. And of course the various commanders would be sorting through all they'd seen, trying to process it while figuring out their next move. Dulce Base might be destroyed, but the alien threat to their planet was still very much a reality.

Anderholt scoffs to himself as the thoughts run through his head. *If only they knew*, he thinks, *if only they knew the truth of it all.*

As the last of the men leave – including Ellis, whom he knows is the real problem, along with that damn son of his – Anderholt takes a side exit and uses the back hallways to get back to his office, or at least the one he's using on the base. As planned, Aaron and Carl are there waiting for him.

"If I gotta sit through another one of these bullshit briefings *or* debriefings then I think I'll shoot myself," Aaron says. He's still in his combat fatigues from the attack on Dulce.

"Make that two of us," Carl says, rolling his eyes.

"That'll be the last of 'em," Anderholt says as he comes into the room and makes his way to his desk. "By tonight everything will be in place. Most of the men that were with you in Dulce will be dead or imprisoned while the Reptilians and Grays will have started their expansion to the surface."

"Yeah, and what about the Dutchman, or that damn son of his?" Aaron says. "You know that once Mark starts talking to his father, everything could change. I mean…who knows *what* he's seen and heard during these last few years off-world. Hell, I thought the bastard went down in Vietnam!"

"We all did," Anderholt says, "we all did."

"So now what?" Carl asks.

"Simple – we take them out."

Aaron frowns to that. "Mark, yeah…but *the Dutchman?* Hell – Ellis is a *legend* in the service. You can't just take him out. What we need to do is get the Dutchman *in on this*, always have!"

Aaron says the words forcefully and with conviction, but Anderholt only scoffs.

"You know Ellis will never come over, will never see things our way – he's too much of a patriot!"

"And that's why we should kill him and be done with it," Carl says. "Having his damn son show up again out of the blue like that just makes things worse."

"Yeah, what *is* the story behind Mark's sudden reappearance?" Aaron asks.

Anderholt shakes his head. "Another time, "then looks to Carl. "And for now, we keep Ellis alive, you got that? His death would create too many questions, get too many balls rolling." He shakes his head. "If that happens there's no saying what'll take place, or how far things will get away from us before we can pull them back."

"Alright, alright," Carl says, his hands up defensively, "no killing." He shrugs. "I will run into him later, though, so maybe another talk is in order."

Anderholt chuckles. "Yeah, like that'll do any good. About as good as the countless other talks you've had with him."

"Maybe we should just come clean with him finally," Aaron says.

"Never," Anderholt says, slamming a fist down on the desk. "If Ellis ever knew the truth, he'd tell everyone…and if that didn't get the results he wanted he'd go to the press."

"Which is why I say we just kill him and be done with it, his son too," Carl says, then puts those hands up again, "but I know you don't want to, so fine, *fine!*"

Anderholt frowns. "What's the matter, Carl? Has Mark's reappearance really shaken you up that bad?"

"And it hasn't shaken you up? Carl nearly shouts. "General…Mark knows *everything* when it comes to what's happening off-world."

"But he doesn't know what's happening on this base," Anderholt replies, "nor will he. And if he ever tries to run, well…he'll turn out just like the survivors of the 1975 attack did."

Aaron narrows his eyes to that, looking over at the general. "But I thought no more than just that one, single survivor had managed to get away."

Anderholt shakes his head. "Nope, all told nineteen escaped back into the tunnels, and since the attack occurred on Level 2, it meant they had a good chance of getting out. Twelve managed to do so. To this day they're still in hiding, crashing in motels and surfing couches, but alive, and safe…and ready to fight in any way they can."

"*God!*" Carl says, a hand going to his forehead. "Let's hope to hell that Ellis doesn't get his hands on 'em."

"The team he's put together is already dangerous enough," Anderholt replies. "I still remember the first time I saw 'em all. *Shit*, they could really put a wrench in things."

"But they won't," Carl says. "We've just got to hang on until tonight, and then it's over, the Reptilians will take charge."

"Getting to tonight will be the hard part," Anderholt replies.

"Not if I keep my eye on Ellis, as well as his son," Carl says, starting to rise. Aaron, sensing that this meeting is over, begins to do the same.

"You do that," Anderholt says as they move toward the door, and then quickly before they leave, "and Carl…"

"Yes, sir?"

"Don't fuck this up."

Carl nods. "No chance, sir."

Anderholt picks up one of his half-burnt cigar stubs as the men leave and then leans back in his chair. He only wishes that what Carl had just said would turn out to be the truth. He knows full-well that it will not, however. Thankfully he still has Heather.

37 – BLUE LAKE REDUX

Blue Lake
Friday, May 25, 1979
6:45 AM

Bobbie and Emil race down the hallways of Blue Lake, hoping they can make it to Ellis's room in time. Bobbie had time-shedded in a short time before, found Chargin' Charlie and quite a few of the others, and just laid it on 'em. It hadn't gone over too well at first, but with persistence Bobbie had convinced them that, yes, the Trifecta was indeed in full swing. After that a quick explanation of what was to come followed, and then Bobbie said he needed one good man. Emil had stepped forward, that ever-present tobacco pipe of his wedged firmly between his teeth and puffing away. Bobbie had nodded, and now both were racing down the hallways, trying to save the Dutchman.

And then they were there, at his door.

"This is it…you ready?" Bobbie asks Emil.

The lieutenant colonel nods and puffs away on that pipe of his while bringing up his Heckler & Koch HK MP5 submachine gun. "The big dog's *always* ready to eat."

Bobbie nods. "Then let's do this."

~~~

Inside Ellis's room, Carl begins to chuckle, and then laugh. "Oh,
~~~

Ellis…*scare you?*" He laughs again. "We're not gonna scare you…we're gonna kill you."

Ellis's eyes narrow and his brow furrows. His heart begins to race and pump adrenaline into his system, and as the flight-or-flight response kicks in, Ellis wonders what he's gotten himself into, and how. Before he can get another question in, however, Carl is reaching into his pants pocket. Ellis's eyes go wide as his friend pulls out a flash gun.

"I'm sorry, Ellis," Carl says as he points the weapon at the Dutchman, "you were always a good friend to me."

Ellis puts his hands up in a 'wait' kind of gesture. "Carl, you don't have to–"

BANG!

Ellis's eyes jerk to the door as it bangs open, kicked open most likely. *Did Carl lock it after he came in?* Ellis wonders, but only for a brief moment. As the door bangs open it strikes Carl in the back, sending him flying down to the floor. That's when the flashgun flies from his hand to skitter across the floor. Ellis watches it slide for a moment, then his eyes shoot back to the door, and the two men coming through it, guns raised.

"Bobbie…Emil!"

"Good to see you too, sir," Emil says as he comes in, his machine gun leading the way. On the floor before him is Carl, moaning slightly but starting to get up. Emil lowers his machine gun's muzzle down to the back of Carl's head.

"No!" Bobbie says loudly, nearly shouting. "We can't kill him – he's got to be alive to get killed *later*, when we rescue Mark."

"Oh, *right*," Emil says, and then instead of firing off a shot like he'd planned, he flips the machine gun around in his hands and slams the butt-end of it down onto the back of Carl's head. He then backs away from Carl, who's now laying there unconscious on the floor.

"Rescue Mark?" Ellis says, looking at Bobbie with confusion written all over his face.

Bobbie rolls his eyes. "We don't have time to explain now," he says, grabbing Ellis by the arm and heading toward the door, "let's just say that after Carl killed you – which he did back there, by the way – then he tries to pin the murder on Mark."

"Pin the murder…?" Ellis begins, trailing-off as Bobbie gets to the door and lets go of him, the better to stick his head out and look both ways down the long hallway.

"Heavy, right?" Emil says from behind Ellis, putting a hand on his back to nudge him forward a bit. "I don't understand the half of it, myself, but you gotta admit that Carl back there…well…"

"Well what?" Bobbie says from the doorway, looking back in. "Carl was gonna kill you and you know it. Now let's go while the coast is clear and–"

Bobbie never finishes the sentence. He's halfway through it – and halfway through the door – when a loud 'blast' sounds and from further down the hall. Both Ellis and Emil watch in shocked horror as Bobbie is ripped apart, almost like a sawed-off shotgun hit him and blew most of his chest and throat and even some of his face away.

"Get back!" Ellis shouts without hesitation, putting his arms up backing up.

"Outta the way, sir!" Emil says from behind him, and instead of being shoved out of the way he moves around Ellis and forward, bringing up his machine gun all the while. He glances over his shoulder as he's past, blowing out a puff of smoke as he does so. "No offense, sir, but I've got this," – he holds up the machine gun – "and you ain't got diddly-squat!"

Ellis can't argue with that so he shrugs and cocks his head to one side. Ahead of him Emil nods and turns back to the door, and the mess that remains of Bobbie that's still visible out in the hallway. He's halfway there when a figure jumps out, right into the doorway, and with his flash gun aimed right at Emil.

BOOM!

The sound is loud, deafening almost in the close confines of Ellis's quarters. Emil does a good job getting his gun up and he even gets a shot off, though it hits the wall beside the door. The figure in the doorway's shot doesn't miss, however, and slams into Emil with the same force and intensity as it'd slammed into Bobbie, though this time at a much closer range. The shot goes through Emil, leaving most of his chest and stomach on the back wall. Ellis watches it slide down onto his desk for a moment, then looks past Emil's dead body on the floor – the ever-present pipe still smoking away between his lips – and to the figure in the doorway.

"Harry," he says with a nod.

"Ellis," General Harry Anderholt replies.

"Looks like you foiled our escape."

Anderholt cocks his head to one side, admitting the truth of Ellis's words. "Not that you had any idea what was going on."

"What *is* going on?"

"Oh, I guess now's the part where I tell you *exactly* what's going to happen, is that it?" Anderholt says, then chuckles as he brings up the flash gun.

Ellis frowns. "Harry…why?"

"Oh, Ellis…don't you know you can't win? Don't you know you can't beat them?"

"So the answer is to join them instead?"

"I would like it if you did, Ellis," Anderholt says, lowing the flash gun slightly, "I'd like that very much."

"You already knew the answer to that before you came here – never."

Anderholt shrugs. "Have it your way."

He brings up the flash gun again, and Ellis doesn't flinch.

BOOM!

Anderholt stands there for a few moments, watching Ellis's insides slide down the wall and onto the desk…but only for a few.

He shrugs. "Just wasn't your time, Ellis."

Then with a disgusted sigh – both of relief and regret – he turns on his heels and leaves the room, closing the door on his way out.

38 – PAYBACK

Blue Lake
Friday, May 25, 1979
6:45 AM

Chargin' Charlie, John, Moses and David rush down the hallways of Blue Lake.

Charlie had managed to scare-up the three to aid him, and when he'd mentioned that the Grays might have a traitor in the base, well…they were all for it. Charlie did a bit of quick explaining – though he wasn't real sure of everything that was going on himself, only what Bobbie had told him and what he knew of the Trifecta – so he was still explaining things as they ran.

"It's a tricky little affair," Charlie calls out as they turn down yet another of the long hallways. "First, Bobbie's got to get to Blue Lake *this morning*, before the Dutchman is killed. After that *we've* got to get to the exact time that Aaron comes back from that Gray mothership that Bobbie says Mark and the others saw him on."

"And how the hell are we gonna do that?" David calls out. Ahead of him, Moses stops dead in his tracks.

"Whoa, what the hell!" Charlie then shouts, but Moses is lost in thought. The words that Stu had told him in the hallway earlier that morning are running through his head.

"*Moses, for the love of God, remember that Aaron gets back just after midnight.*"

"Het gets back just after midnight," Moses says, turning around with a smile on his face. "Aaron gets back just after midnight!"

"And how the hell you know that, huh?" David asks.

"Stu told me this morning."

The men narrow their eyes to that, but say nothing. Strange things are happening, and if Moses knows the time, well…it's a helluva lot more than the rest of 'em know.

"If Stu said it then it's good enough for me," Charlie replies, then looks at them all. "Let's get to the time shed."

~~~

Blue Lake
Friday, May 25, 1979
12:02 AM

Charlie looks down at his watch, then over at Moses. "Just after midnight…now what?"

"Now we wait, what else?" David says before the pilot can answer.

Moses nods to that so Charlie does as well. The other two men just shrug and wait. They'd gotten to the time shed room by running down the hallways of Blue Lake and getting to the basement.

The room is like a storage room, and it looks the part. Boxes are piled nearly up to the ceiling against one wall, while a table pushed up against another wall is also covered with them. The only thing that looks out of place is a large, rectangular box standing at one side of the room. If it wasn't for all the wires and tubes going into it, the men might have guessed it was some kind of shower stall, though one without a working faucet or shower head. It's the time shed, looking old and dusty and hardly used. It doesn't really look like a shed so much as a space pod of some sort, complete with a window on the door and a seat inside where you sat, waiting for it all to happen once you hit the controls. There was another control panel on the outside of the shed, which allowed someone to set the time destination from outside.

After that they'd all gotten into the room Charlie had switched the controls to shoot them to just before midnight that morning, or what was about 7 hours earlier than where (or when) they'd just been.

"I hope the others are doin' alright," David says after a few
~~~

moments of silence have passed.

"They're set," Charlie says, turning around to look at the others. "Donlon and Stu will have just gotten Tommy's body into the morgue – *their* angle is set. Now, I've been thinkin' about our situation here…" he says, grinning a bit and slapping one of his Colt .45's down in his hand, "how 'bout some payback for that traitorous bastard Aaron?"

"Now you're talkin'!" David nearly shouts while beside him John says, "Not sure one helping'll be enough – how 'bout we use the time machines to go back and kill him twice?"

"Oh, *we're* not gonna kill him," Charlie says.

"Wait…what'dya mean?" David says, and several of the others echo the comment.

"I got a better idea, a *lot* better," Charlie replies, and then stands there, crossing his arms and enjoying the look of confusion on the men's faces.

"You wanna fill us in?" John asks.

"Yeah, what's this all about?"

"Well boys, you remember the Lake Oswego Incident a few years back?"

"Ha!" Moses laughs. "How can we forget?"

"You don't forget something like that," David says.

"And I'm sure Aaron hasn't either," Charlie says, "it's just today…he'll be getting a front row seat to it."

The men's eyes go wide at that. If Charlie was going to do what they thought he was, then his reputation as one bad ass motherfucker was cemented in their minds, oh yes indeed!

~~~

A few minutes later a shimmering curtain of light appears within the time shed, though that's not quite right either. If Charlie and the others hiding behind the crates and boxes had to describe it they'd say it was like looking at one of those rain puddles you'd see at a gas station, an oil sheen floating at the top and giving the water a purplish, greenish sort of look.

Then there's a flash from within the shed, and through the window the men can see movement. It's Aaron.

Inside the machine Aaron is eager to get out and find General
~~~

Anderholt so he can tell him about Mark and Bennewitz being on the mothership. He's about ready to open the door when movement outside the shed's window catches his eye. Then a person is there at the window, and Aaron knows exactly who it is.

"Charlie!" he says, his mouth twisting into a sneer. It quickly morphs into a smile, however, for he's already safe – he just has to hit the controls. He reaches forth to do so.

"I wouldn't do that if I were you," Charlie says quickly through the glass, nearly yelling to be heard through its thickness.

That stalls Aaron, but only for a moment. His hand continues toward the appropriate buttons to push.

"You ain't goin' to that mothership!" Carl then shouts, and that does stop Aaron. The master sergeant looks up, his eyes narrowing in skeptical confusion. Charlie nods toward the controls. "Look at the time."

Aaron narrows his eyes and stares intently at the control panel that Charlie has just motioned to, and which he himself was just ready to touch. Then he sees the date, and his eyes widen and dart to Charlie.

"No," he says.

"What?" Charlie replies.

"Not that time, anywhere but there…*anywhere*!"

"Oh, so you can dish it out but you can't take it, eh?" Charlie says. "More than 50,000 died at Lake Oswego, and Portland was nearly engulfed. That whole timeline was disrupted, and word is that the Collective deems it worthless now." Charlie shakes his head, glancing down at the floor before meeting Aaron's eyes once again. "The Lake Oswego Incident was your doing, Aaron…and now you'll get a taste of it firsthand." He looks over to David and nods. "Hit it."

David nods to that and does indeed hit it, banging his fist against the controls. The machine immediately starts to life, and sparks and mini bolts of lighting begin to crackle about.

"No!" Aaron shouts. "No, you can't do this! Nnnnoooo!!!!"

That last shout is drawn-out, not because Aaron makes it that way, but because the time shed has fired to life. It pulls Aaron from their time and puts him back in a different one, one that was set by Charlie and showing on the control panel.

"Helluva way to die," John says.

"Who says he's gonna die?" Moses replies. "After all, we left him his machine gun and his knife."

"Same knife he used to kill Johnny," Charlie says.

David scoffs. "We'll see how many Grays he can take out with the thing.

The men stare at the controls for a short time after that, wondering how Aaron would fare.

39 – THE LAKE OSWEGO INCIDENT

Lake Oswego in Portland, Oregon
Monday, April 2, 1956
8:12 PM

Mini bolts of lighting crackle and spark, and a short distance over the parking lot, a shimmering portal appears. It holds there for a moment, then a faint sound begins to come through.

"Nnnnoooo…*ugh!*"

The sound stops as Aaron hits the pavement, the wind nearly getting knocked out of him. He coughs a few times and then begins to brush himself off as he gets up. He clutches his machine gun protectively, and holds his knife in his hand as well, loosening and tightening his fingers to help ease his worry. And he has a lot to worry about.

My God, he thinks*, I'm really in Lake Oswego.*

The suburb of Portland, Oregon, had over 4,000 people and is often tagged as 'Lake No-Negro' by the upscale locals, most of whom are rich and the kind that relished looking down on those who were not. Aaron knew this, for he'd grown up just outside the area, in Beaverton. He'd always wanted to be a part of the better community, but he couldn't be – his parents were too poor. So he began to despise the place instead. Perhaps that's what brought him to choose the suburb for one of his experiments, one that MJ12 signed-off on back in 1952. And oh, how it'd gone terribly wrong.

It's all the command sergeant can do to just collapse to his knees, his gun and his knife in his hand as he stares forth at the carnage around him. People lie dead everywhere while nearly every building and tree in sight burns.

Aaron catches a tune on the air then, and looks over to see a TV in the distance. The command sergeant didn't have to look too hard to know what was on it, either.

"April 2," he chuckles, knowing the date, "Goddamn soap operas!"

The tune continues, the opening theme to *As the World Turns*, debuting that very day. It was the Grays' first attempt at mass-mind-control, and *oh*, Aaron thought, *how wondrous that had turned out for them!* By the 1970s millions were watching it each day, and having their will to live sapped along the way. The was the one glitch left over from the Lake Oswego Incident, that damn TV show.

The Grays behind Aaron crept closer, taking their time. There were hundreds of them around, and just one of Aaron. They knew his name alright, were reading his thoughts that very moment. He knew he was dead, and they knew he'd been betrayed. He wasn't the first to get sent here to this alternate time loop that'd been cut-off from the universe, a discarded shard, an experimental mistake. But it existed still, and the Grays here relished their few opportunities to mete out a little payback for the pointless existence they had here.

Aaron continues to stare forward, while behind him the first of the large skyscrapers in downtown Portland begins to fall. He hears it, hears the screams of people, then the crash and the steady rumble. Dust and debris is coming up, he knows, much like it did on 9/11 when the twin towers came down. He remembers that day well, thanks to his time with John Titor and the 177th.

Behind him the Grays read all this from his mind, and grow tired of it. They know Titor, they know the 177th, and they don't like knowing either. The Gray closest to Aaron takes the device its been holding at its side and puts it up. It glows and sparks with a sort of crackling lighting. The humans that've seen it in action call it a 'mind warp,' the Gray knows, but to them it's just like a spoon or a fork, a way to feed. Usually it'd be placed over the head or against the forehead, then a low setting would start and some of the spiritual energy would be taken from the human. The Gray wasn't intending to put it on a low setting this day, however. Here in this cut off part of time and space, there was no reason to use discretion.

Reaching out, the Gray put the 'mind warp' above Aaron's head, then switched it on as high as it would go. Aaron jerks in place, as if some invisible hand has just grabbed him. Then he begins to shake, his whole body at first, but then just his upper torso and finally his head. Then it happens. With a loud, *CRUNCH!*, Aaron's head simply caves in on itself. The 'mind warp' keeps his body upright, however, and a moment later a wispy white, ghostlike substance begins to come from that body. It's Aaron's soul, and the Gray gives an inward smile at the psychic cry of agony coming from that soul. Aaron thought he'd simply been going to die. He had no idea he'd be going to a place worse than Hell.

THE END

To Be Concluded…in *Dulce Depths*

BIBLIOGRAPHY

Is Dulce Base real or just complete BS?

I dunno.

I'd *like* to believe it's true, but doing so makes me worry a great deal for our country and for our human race. That said, there's more than enough information out there for you to make up your own mind.

I've used that information to make this book as 'factual' as possible, or at least as much as I can make it when the facts are based in the realm of conspiracy.

Needless to say, Coast to Coast AM with George Noory has been both eye-opening and mind-expanding when it comes to this subject matter, and ufology in general.

If you haven't tuned into that late-night radio talk show yet, I encourage you to do so.

For more information on Dulce, aliens, time travel, and space in general…check out these sources:

"Arcturus." *Wikipedia.* 31 January 2017. Web. Retrieved 16 February 2017. http://en.wikipedia.org/wiki/Arcturus

Booth, Billy. "1991-Russian Crash & Retrieval." *About Entertainment.* Web. Retrieved 16 February 2017. http://ufos.about.com/od/bestufocrashcases/p/russia1991.htm

"Climate Controversies/ET & UFO Contacts." *Coast to Coast AM.* KGVO News Talk Radio: Missoula. 16 March 2017. http://www.coasttocoastam.com/show/2017/03/16

Collier, Alex. "The Greys and the Earth Agenda." *Bibliotecapleyades.* Web. Retrieved 3 March 2017. http://www.bibliotecapleyades.net/andromeda/esp_andromeda com_7aa.htm#

Commander X. *Underground Alien Bases: Flying Saucers Come From Inside The Earth!* Global Communications: New Brunswick, 2012. p 28-38.

"Did President Eisenhower Meet with Aliens at Holloman Air Force Base?" *Gaia.* 21 November 2016. Web. Retrieved 10 March 2017. https://www.gaia.com/article/eisenhower-meets-aliens-holloman-afb

"Dulce, New Mexico." *Wikipedia.* 24 February 2017. Web. Retrieved 3 March 2017. https://en.wikipedia.org/wiki/Dulce,_New_Mexico

"Epsilon Boötis." *Wikipedia.* 31 January 2017. Web. Retrieved 16 February 2017. http://en.wikipedia.org/wiki/Epsilon_Bo%C3%B6tis

"Giordano Bruno (crater)." *Wikipedia.* 22 May 2016. Web. Retrieved 16 February 2017. http://en.wikipedia.org/wiki/Giordano_Bruno_(crater)

"Is Lumley's UFO still out there? (1865)" Above Top Secret. Web. 6 December 2008. Retrieved 2 April 2017. http://www.abovetopsecret.com/forum/thread417392/pg1

"Jicarilla Apache." *Wikipedia.* 11 December 2016. Web. Retrieved 3 March 2017. https://en.wikipedia.org/wiki/Jicarilla_Apache

"John Titor." *Wikipedia.* 3 March 2017. Web. Retrieved 3 March 2017. https://en.wikipedia.org/wiki/John_Titor

"John Titor II, Biography." *Coast to Coast AM.* 1 September 2016. Web. Retrieved 3 March 2017. http://www.coasttocoastam.com/guest/titor-ii-john/81682

"Reptilian Conquest." *Coast to Coast AM.* KGVO News Talk Radio: Missoula. 11 March 2017. http://www.coasttocoastam.com/show/2017/03/11

Schwarz, Rob. "The Time Travel and Teleportation Experiments of Project Pegasus." *Stranger Dimensions.* 13 February 2014. Web. Retrieved 3 March 2017. http://www.strangerdimensions.com/2014/02/13/time-travel-teleportation-experiments-project-pegasus/

"The Black Knight Satellite, Bracewell Probes, and Philip K. Dick." *Mysterious Universe.* 21 February 2014. Web. Retrieved 16 February 2017. http://mysteriousuniverse.org/2014/02/the-black-knight-satellite-bracewell-probes-and-phillip-k-dick/

"The CIA Has a Secret Time Travel Program, But They Won't Let us Know About It." 21 February 2016. Web. Retrieved 3 March 2017. http://ufoholic.com/conspiracy/the-cia-has-a-secret-time-travel-program-but-they-wont-let-us-know-about-it/

"The Dulce Base Code: J.B. III." *Truth CDM.* Web. Retrieved 3 March 2017. http://truthcdm.com/dulce-base-code-j-b-ill/

"Uncovering the True Story of Paul F. Bennewitz." *Above Top Secret.* Web. 24 April 2011. Retrieved 4 March 2017. http://www.abovetopsecret.com/forum/thread693727/pg1

Other Exciting Books by Greg Strandberg

Montana's paranormal history comes alive from the time of the Indians all the way to 2016. Learn about UFOs, cattle mutilations, Bigfoot sightings, lake monsters, Indian myths, and lots of other strange things in Paranormal Montana!

20 sci-fi short stories for just $0.99! Topics range from nuclear apocalypse, alien contact, economic chaos, killer cosmetics, secret space programs, shadow governments and more!

It's June 1973 in Hong Kong. Inspector Jim Sharpe is drinking heavily and about to be brought up on charges of corruption. To save his career he'll need to tackle the most difficult case of his life, one his superiors may be in on. It all depends on who the *Tarot Card Killer* is.

It's 1806 and mountain man John Colter is ready to leave the Lewis and Clark Expedition. He gets his chance when a pair of fur trappers come up the Missouri River. What he doesn't know is that those fur trappers have a dark secret, one that will turn these hunters into the hunted. Find out what happens in *Colter's Winter*.

What really happened to Flight 370? Did it just disappear or was there a vast government conspiracy involved? Find out in this thrilling adventure novel that speculates on one of the greatest mysteries of our time.

Ernie Tanner is slow, but he's not stupid. That's why when his and the boys' pensions are stolen by fat cat bankers, Ernie knows what to do. It involves guns and vengeance, and that's exactly what you get with *Wake Up, Detroit*!

It's been six months since the horrendous incident atop Mount Misery, the incident that broke Beldar Thunder Hammer's band of adventurers apart. Now Beldar's putting the band back together. Why? To head back up Mount Misery to end the Kingdom's Hireling system for good. A tale of epic fantasy adventure unfolds, one you won't want to miss!

1075 AD. William the Conqueror's army sits outside Norwich Castle, the siege of three months going nowhere fast. The men need ale, but there is none. One man can get it for them, Sir Peter Godfried. He sets out, and along the way he finds love, trouble, laughs, and a hideous plot to upend the kingdom in this humorous and edgy historical novella.

ABOUT THE AUTHOR

Greg Strandberg was born and raised in Helena, Montana, and graduated from the University of Montana in 2008 with a BA in History. He lived and worked in China following the collapse of the American economy. After five years he moved back to Montana where he now lives with his wife and young son. He's written more than 80 books.

www.bigskywords.com

Made in the USA
Las Vegas, NV
09 August 2022

52955022R10111